ERICH VON GOTHA

A VERY SPECIAL PRISON

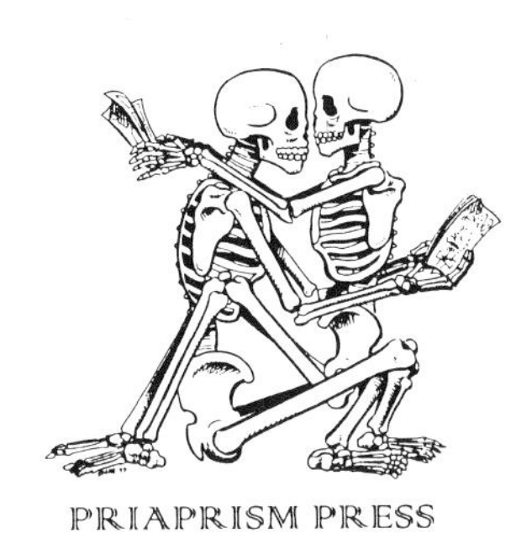

PRIAPRISM PRESS

A VERY SPECIAL PRISON

ISBN 0-86719-449-9

Published in the United States by
Last Gasp of San Francisco, P.O. Box 410067
San Francisco, Ca 94141-0067

Originally published in France as *Une Prison Très Spéciale* by
International Presse Magazine
All models are over 18 years of age.
Dealers are instructed not to sell this book to minors.

Translated by Georgina Ranuzzi

Printed in Spain

BUT, WESTON, YOU KNOW THAT TIM HIMSELF PUT THE HEROIN IN MY BAG...

THAT'S WHAT YOU TOLD ME, EMMA..

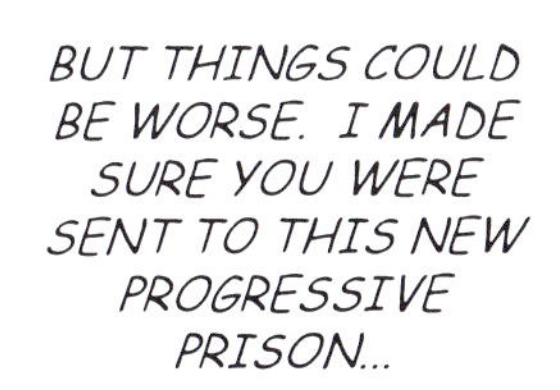

WAY AHEAD OF ITS TIME..."

THEN LATER...

WELL!... WHAT A PECULIAR PRISON...

YOUR ATTENTION! DO AS YOU ARE TOLD AT EVERY MOMENT, MCALISTAIR...AND YOU'LL FIND THIS PLACE NICE ENOUGH TO SPEND YOUR TIME...NOW..

COME IN... DROP YOUR BAGS...

AND TAKE OFF YOUR CLOTHES...

I WANT TO SEE YOUR BODY...
?

YOU ARE SO GOOD LOOKING AND SEXY.. IN FACT, YOU... WILL BE PERFECT FOR OUR PURPOSES...
PURPOSES?!.

WHAT..?!

AH! THE NEW ONE!.. A LITTLE REBEL, AIN'T SHE?
BUT!..

MY GOD! I CAN'T BELIEVE IT! A MALE GUARD IN A WOMAN'S JAIL!...

KEEP QUIET! YOU ARE IN A NEW TYPE OF JAIL.
>GASP< >CHOKE<

WE'LL MAKE SURE YOU'LL LIKE IT...
BUT ALL THIS IS...
HIGHLY ILLEGAL!!

SHUT UP FOR NOW! SIMM! PUT SOME CHAINS ON HER AND TAKE OFF HER STOCK-INGS...
MY GOD!!

...YOU CAN'T GET AWAY WITH THIS!
SILLY GIRL! SIMM! THE WHIP!

WITH PLEASURE, SIR!
THE WHIP, BUT...
WHIP HER, SIMM!!

WHI...I...

WHIP!
GOOD LORD!

NOO! AOH!

NOOOOOO!
KLAK!

PLEASE, HAVE MERCY, STOP! I WON'T TELL.. I BEG OF YOU...

I'LL DO ANY-THING!
...IT'S INCREDIBLE...
BUT, STOP
WHAT DO YOU WANT?...
Erich von Götha 1989
5

OH! HAVE MERCY! MY GOD! MERCY!

?!
SLUT! UHN!

IT MUST BE A BAD DREAM
YOU DRENCHED HER BELLY! I LOVE YOU...HMM..LET ME LICK IT, MY MASTER...

OH... AH...

MY DEAR MASTER...YOUR COME IS SO... BUT...?

MY GOD SHE'S WET WITH HER OWN JUICE.. SHE LIKES IT! MAYBE THE SLUT LIKES TO SUCK..

..DICKS ALSO!
!!

BUT IT'S A NIGHT-MARE!

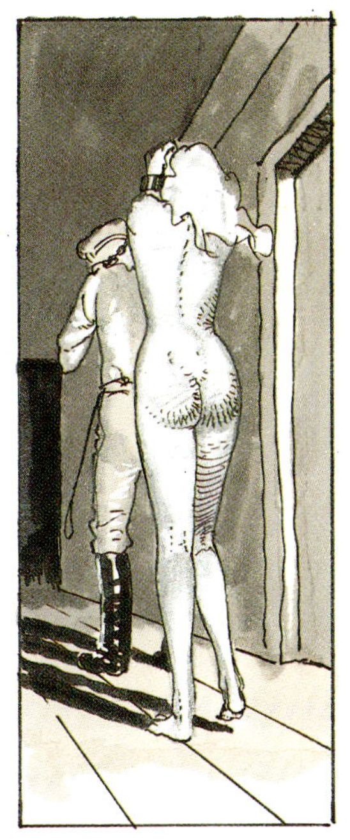

AS IN A DREAM, EMMA WENT THROUGH REGISTRATION THEN WENT TO SLEEP. SUDDENLY..

IT'S TRUE! DID THEY CALL YOUR MOM TO TELL HER YOU ARE ALL RIGHT? YES?
YES! SHE'S BEEN TOLD...

THEY SAID SHE'D COME SOON..
THAT MEANS THEY'LL ACT SOON..

ANNOUNCE YOUR ESCAPE IN THE PRESS.
WHAT ARE THEY GOING TO DO? OH DON'T DO THIS!

MY ESCAPE?
YOUR ESCAPE.. HMMM..

OH, MY GOD, I..I..
YES, YES.. AAH, OH..

AND YOUR FINAL DISAPPEAR-ANCE!

WHAT ARE YOU TWO DOING? COME HERE, SLUT! COME ON! MOVE YOUR ASS!!

HOW DARE YOU SPEAK TO ME LIKE THIS?

COME ON! IT'S TIME FOR YOUR EXAM!
EXAM??!
WHAT DO YOU MEAN?
CLIK!

SHUT UP!!
NO NEED TO RESIST! THE RESULTS SHOW THAT YOU WERE BORN TO BE A SLAVE... TODAY WE CHECK!.
A SLAVE! THIS IS SHEER CRAZINESS!

MCALISTAIR! READY FOR HER EXAMS!
WE WERE WAIT-ING... WE EXPECT YOUR EXAMS TO BE UNCOMMON.

WHAT DOES THIS MEAN? I WANT TO KNOW...

SHUT UP, SLAVE! SORRY MA'M, SHE'S A DIFFICULT ONE, THIS ONE... I THINK SHE NEEDS SOME DISCIPLINE...
?!!

SHE'LL GET SOME! OFFICER HODDLE.. PRISONER MCALISTAIR 73C B9.
OK! SEND HER IN!

COME..
!
H'M HOWYA SLUT!
UNBELIEV-ABLE

THIS IS AN OUTRAGE!!
SHUT UP, STUPID! YOUR OBSERVATIONS ARE OF NO INTEREST TO ANYBODY!
H'MMM.. THIS ONE IS GOING TO BE TROUBLE!

GOOD.. A NEW ONE.. GOOD
SHE'S AN EASY ONE, THIS ONE..
IS THIS A REAL PRISON?
TOO EASY FOR YOU..

HELP!
MY GOD!

SO HUMILIATING! THERE I AM, NAKED.. BEING EXPOSED IN THOSE HALLS LIKE AN ANIMAL.. NAKED.. DEFENSELESS.. ON A LEASH..

COME IN!
WHY DOES THIS TURN ME ON?

MY GOD, HE'S A BRUTE!
MCALISTAIR, OFFICER HODDLE. I SURPRISED HER ENGAGED WITH SOMEBODY ELSE...
MALE OR FEMALE?
EXAMINATION ROOM OFF: HODDLE
MALE? MALE PRISONERS, HERE?

WHO CARES? TYPICAL BEHAVIOR OF A SEX SLAVE.. BUT NOW...
HODDLE

NOW! LET'S SEE WHAT YOU CAN DO!
NO!
PLEASE! I BEG YOU...ALL THIS IS HIGHLY ILLEGAL! I'LL COMPLAIN
YOU WON'T COMPLAIN TO ANYBODY - YOU'LL EVEN TASTE THE WHIP!
NO!
OH! HAVE MERCY! STOP! I'LL DO ANY-THING YOU WANT!
HERE! THAT'S BETTER!
LIE DOWN! YOU'LL BE TRUSSED UP LIKE AN ANIMAL READY FOR THE SACRIFICE.. THEN..
LET'S SEE HOW YOU REACT TO THIS,,,
WHY DO YOU DO THIS? WHY? OH! WHAT ARE YOU DOING?.
OH! OUCH! STOP! AHH.AHH..
Erich von Götha
IT'S SO.. OOH.. AAHH..
IT'S INCREDIBLE.. OOH .. I'M COMING.. I .. AAAAH.. YES! YES!
H'MM DELICIOUS, SUPERB.. WE CON-FIRMED IT.. THERE IS NO DOUBT..
IS SHE A BORN SLAVE?
YES, A SEX SLAVE. NOW PASS THE LACTRENE THEN YOU CAN GO, OFFICER.
MMM...
SHUT UP AND DRINK THIS EMMA.

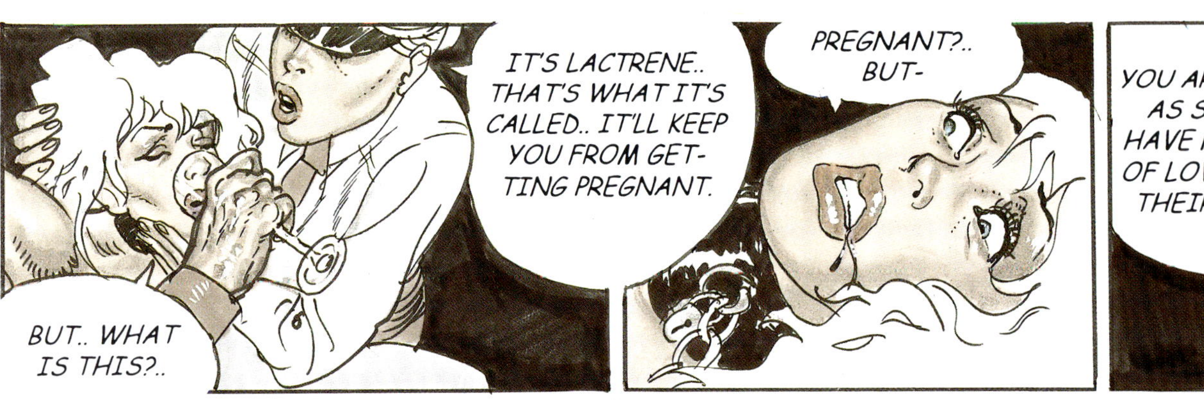
BUT.. WHAT IS THIS?..
IT'S LACTRENE.. THAT'S WHAT IT'S CALLED.. IT'LL KEEP YOU FROM GETTING PREGNANT.
PREGNANT?.. BUT-

YOU ARE A SLAVE! AS SUCH YOU HAVE NO CHOICE OF LOVERS OR OF THEIR NUMBER!

BUT.. WELL..
SORRY, I WAS...

NOW..

NO WASTE... CLEAN WHAT YOU SPIT ON MY DICK.. AH! YOU ARE STARTING WELL...
Erich von Gotha

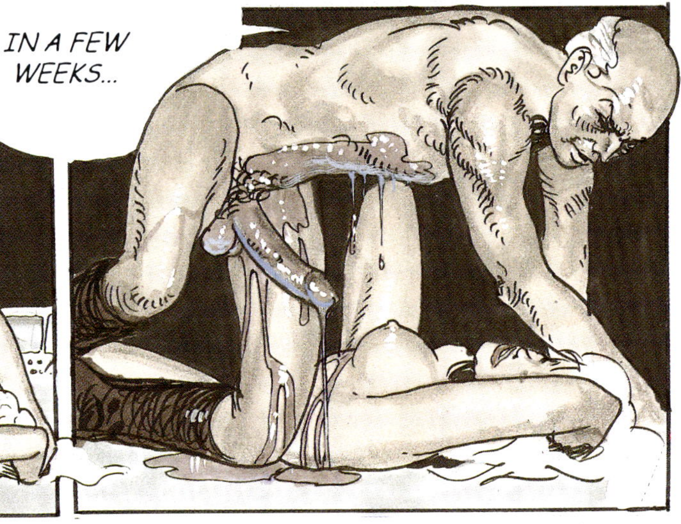
IN A FEW WEEKS...

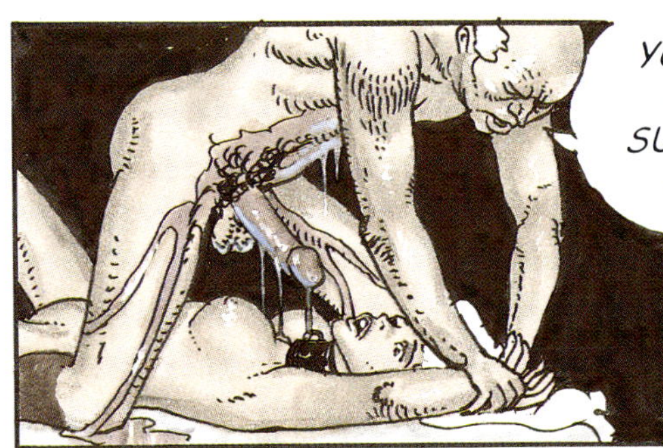

YOU'LL BE THE QUEEN OF SUCKERS.. NOW PRACTICE!!
NO! NO!!!

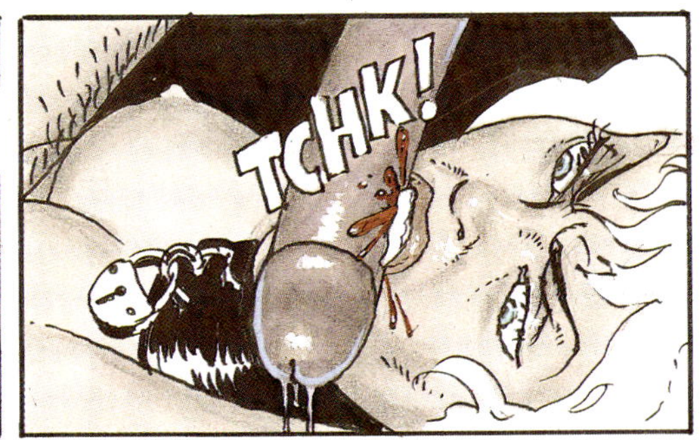
TCHK!

AAH

MY GOD!

WHAT AM I DOING?

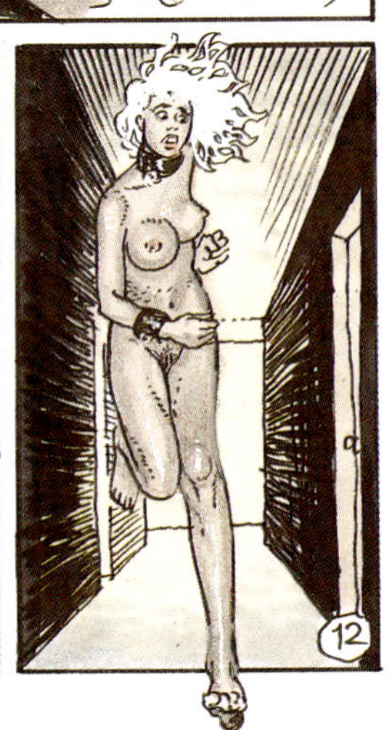

STOP !

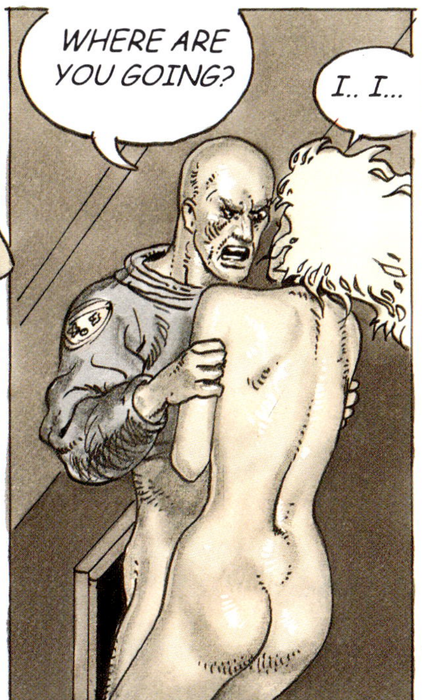
WHERE ARE YOU GOING?
I.. I...

COME!

LATER

A DIFFICULT CASE...

CONTRADICTING HER OWN NATURE..

I WONDER WHY..
DANGEROUS...

BUT THERE'S ONLY ONE WAY FOR YOU, BABE..

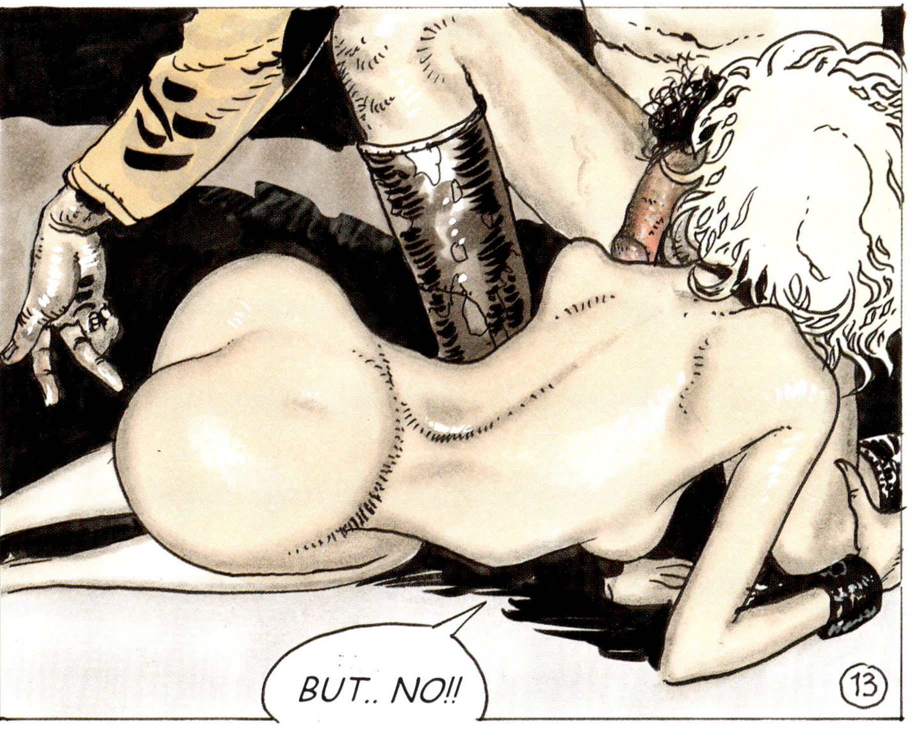
BUT.. NO!!

OUCH! I BEG YOU.. I
SHE LIKES IT, CARRY ON!
NO!.. I...AAAH.. MMM...
YOU LIKE IT, DON'T YOU? SLUT!
I THINK SHE'S COMING...
YESSS! OH,GOD!.. AH,AH, AH! I'M COMING..
SOON YOU'LL ACCEPT BECOMING THE SLAVE YOU'VE ALWAYS WANTED TO BE!
..OR YOU'LL REGRET IT... YOU ARE A DIFFICULT CASE, EMMA...
THERE'S NO PEACE HERE FOR TROUBLEMAKERS LIKE YOU!
LIKE ME?! HOW DARE YOU? I AM INNOCENT! I WAS HAPPY!
Erich von Götha
14

HAPPY! WITH YOUR DREAMS AND MASTURBATIONS...ALONE IN YOUR BED?..
BUT, HOW CAN YOU?..

STARTING LAST NIGHT, WE ELECTRONICALLY RE-CORDED YOUR NIGHTLY DREAMS... WE KNOW YOU ARE A SEX ADDICT .. AND VERY VALUABLE
VALUABLE!! BUT I AM NOT A WHORE!

SHUT UP! YOU HAVE PROSTITUTION FANTASIES!
I HAVE NO MORE SECRETS!
YOUR DREAMS CLAIM YOU ARE A SEX ADDICT!
BUT THEY'RE ONLY DREAMS!
DREAMS ARE DESIRES AND DESIRES ARE WHAT ONE SHOULD LIVE... UNLIKE AN ADDICT LIKE YOU, I CAN CHOOSE...

MY LIFESTYLE.. WHEN YOUR WHOLE LIFE IS DESIGNED IN ADVANCE.. IF ONLY BY YOUR OWN...
PSYCHOLOGICAL REACTIONS!
THAT'S DESTINY! YOU WERE MADE FOR SEX!!

SO! SHOW US YOUR PUSSY! SPREAD YOUR LEGS!
ZTHWHAT!
DO IT! SPREAD 'EM!

YOU'RE LUCKY YOU HAVEN'T BEEN STRANGLED FOR WHAT YOU DID TO THE EXPERT...
A CHOICE? BETWEEN SLAVERY AND DEATH?
AT LEAST, THE JUDGES LEFT YOU A CHOICE

YOU ARE NOT CONCERNED WITH WHAT YOU DID TO HODDLE THE EXPERT?
YES, YES OF COURSE, I...

SAY "HOW DARE YOU" ONE MORE TIME AND WE'LL SHOW YOU HOW WE DARE BE OBEYED!

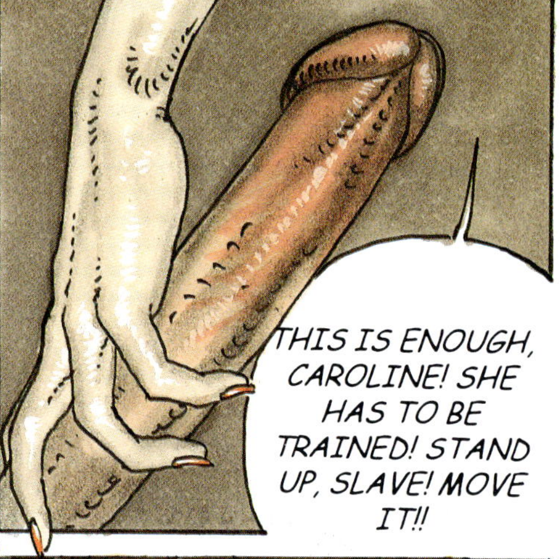

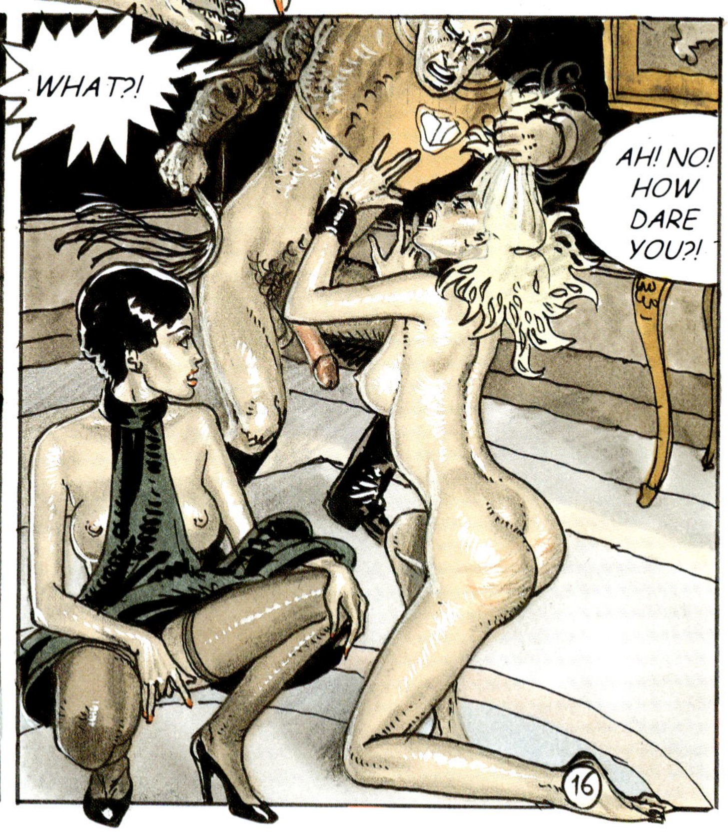

WHAT DID YOU SAY?
HMMMH...

OUCH!
NO! AAAH!
SHLK!

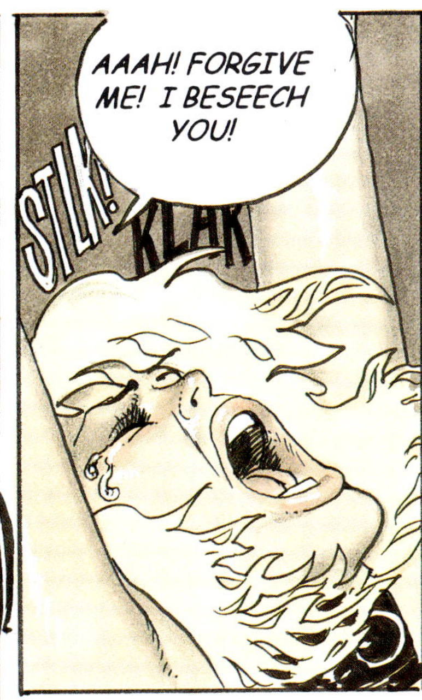
AAAH! FORGIVE ME! I BESEECH YOU!
STLK!
KLAK

YOU ARE HURTING ME! IF I WERE NOT SUCH A NICE GIRL, I'D..
TZK

A NICE GIRL?! AH! YOU! YOU HAVE A LOT TO LEARN... MY NAME IS MOFFATT BUT YOU'LL LEARN TO CALL ME MASTER...
YOU SPARE ME,... MASTER?...

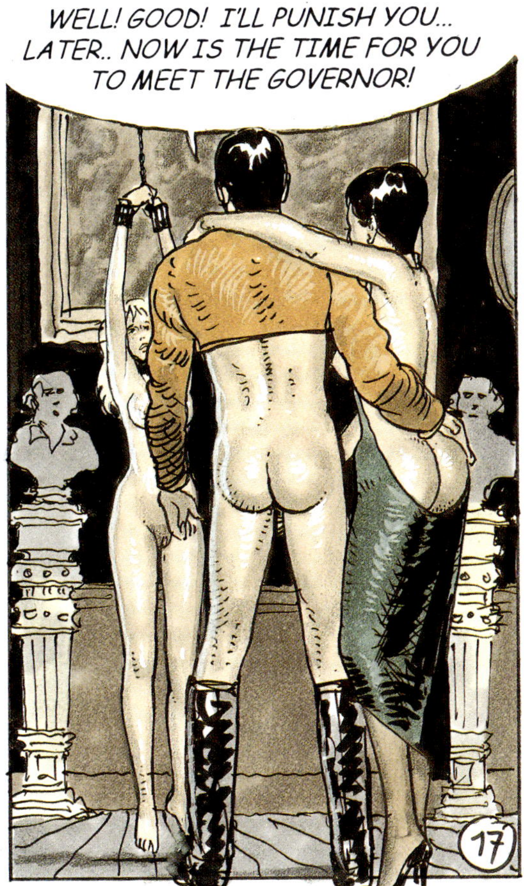
WELL! GOOD! I'LL PUNISH YOU... LATER.. NOW IS THE TIME FOR YOU TO MEET THE GOVERNOR!

THIS WAY, SLUT!!
TOC! TOC!

NUMBER?
CB9 MCALISTAIR, LORD HAMMETT.

AH, YES! THE FAMOUS MCALISTAIR, DICKEATER.. YOU CAN GO, OFFICER MOFFATT! AND WHAT IF I PUT MY DICK IN YOUR MOUTH? COME HERE, SLUT.. I WANT TO...

OH! AH! AAH! AAAH!
MMMM.. YOU'RE WET.. AND FULL OF!!.. YOU HAVE BEEN PLAYED WITH, RECENTLY! IS THIS SPERM?
NO! OF COURSE NOT!

TOO BAD!..
A REBELIOUS STUDENT... I HOPED THAT MAYBE YOU HAD BECOME.. UNDERSTANDING.. STILL..
SINCE YOU DON'T EXIST ANYMORE..
I DON'T EXIST?!
I'LL SHOW YOU THE PAPERS.. NOW I MUST TAKE A DECISION..EITHER I INVEST LARGE AMOUNTS OF MONEY IN YOUR TRAINING...

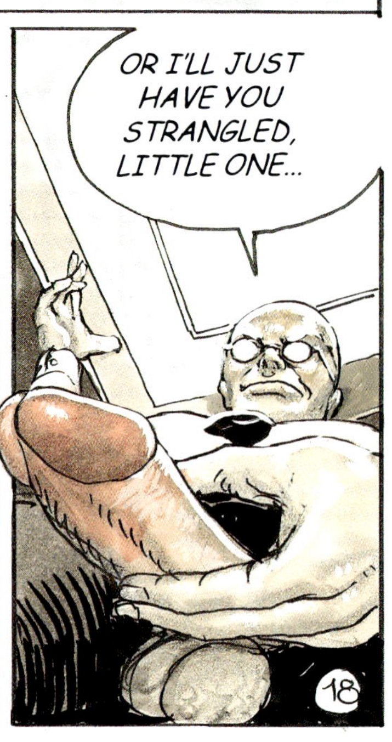
OR I'LL JUST HAVE YOU STRANGLED, LITTLE ONE...

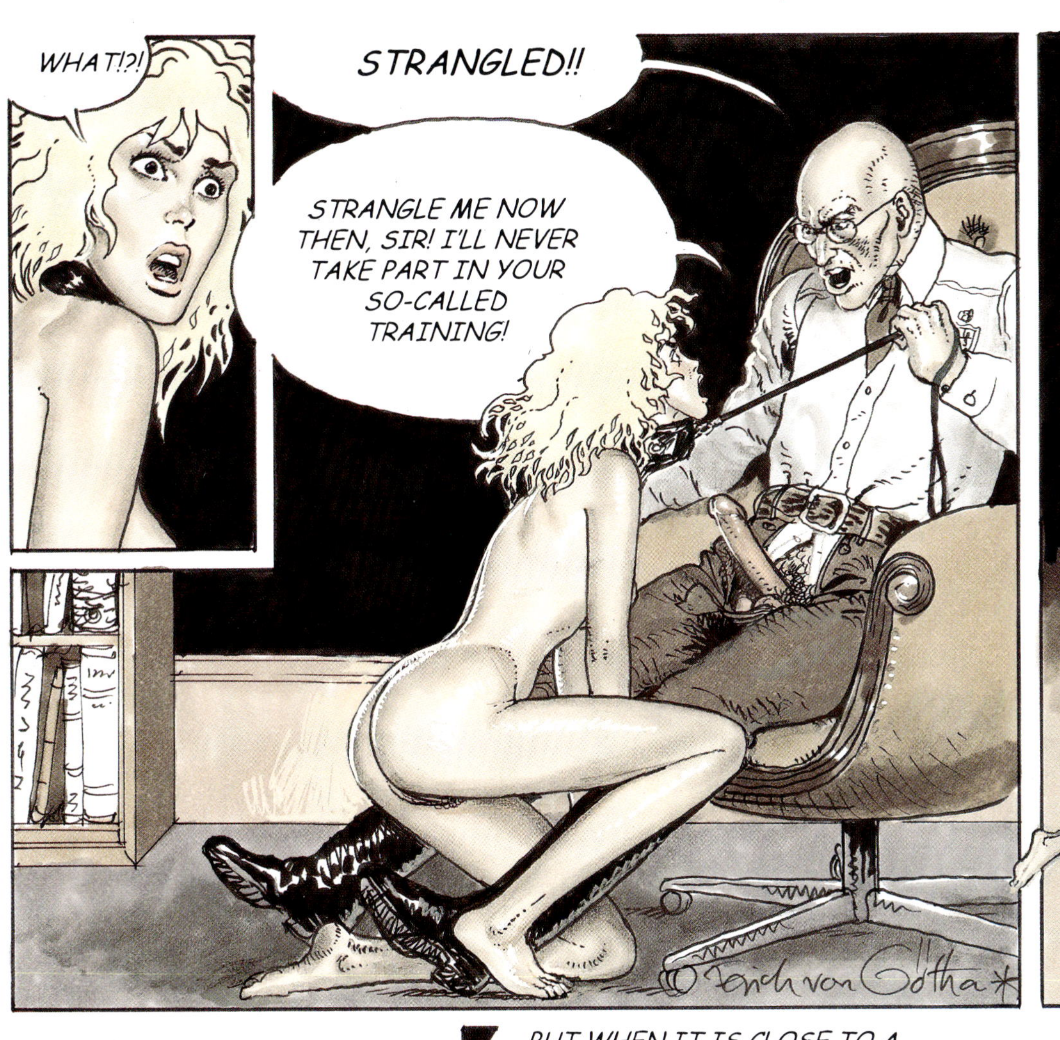
WHAT!?!
STRANGLED!!
STRANGLE ME NOW THEN, SIR! I'LL NEVER TAKE PART IN YOUR SO-CALLED TRAINING!
Erich von Götha

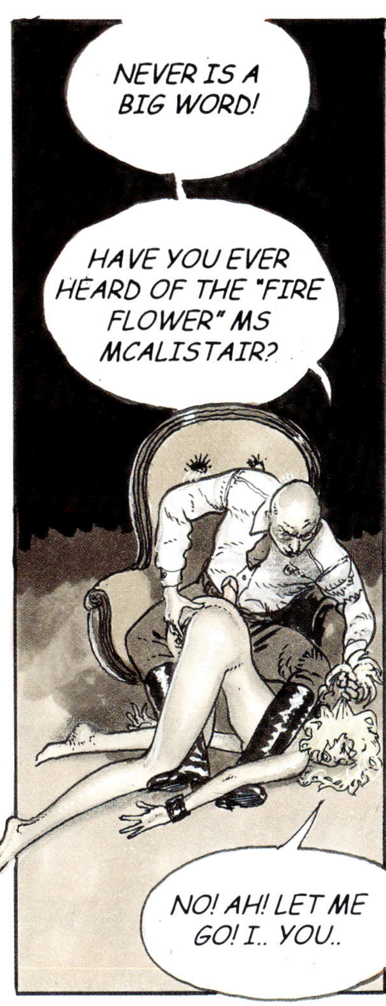
NEVER IS A BIG WORD!
HAVE YOU EVER HEARD OF THE "FIRE FLOWER" MS MCALISTAIR?
NO! AH! LET ME GO! I.. YOU..

IT COMES FROM AFRICA.. IT IS USUALLY OF A GREYISH COLOR..
OUCH!

BUT WHEN IT IS CLOSE TO A MALE, IT BECOMES...
AOH!

BLOOD AND GOLD COL-ORED! AS A BURNING FLAME! SOME SEX AD-DICTS ARE LIKE THAT! THEY BLOOM IN SLAVERY AND WHEN THEY BLOOM, WHEN THEY MATURE,.. THEY ARE CALLED FIREFLOWERS...

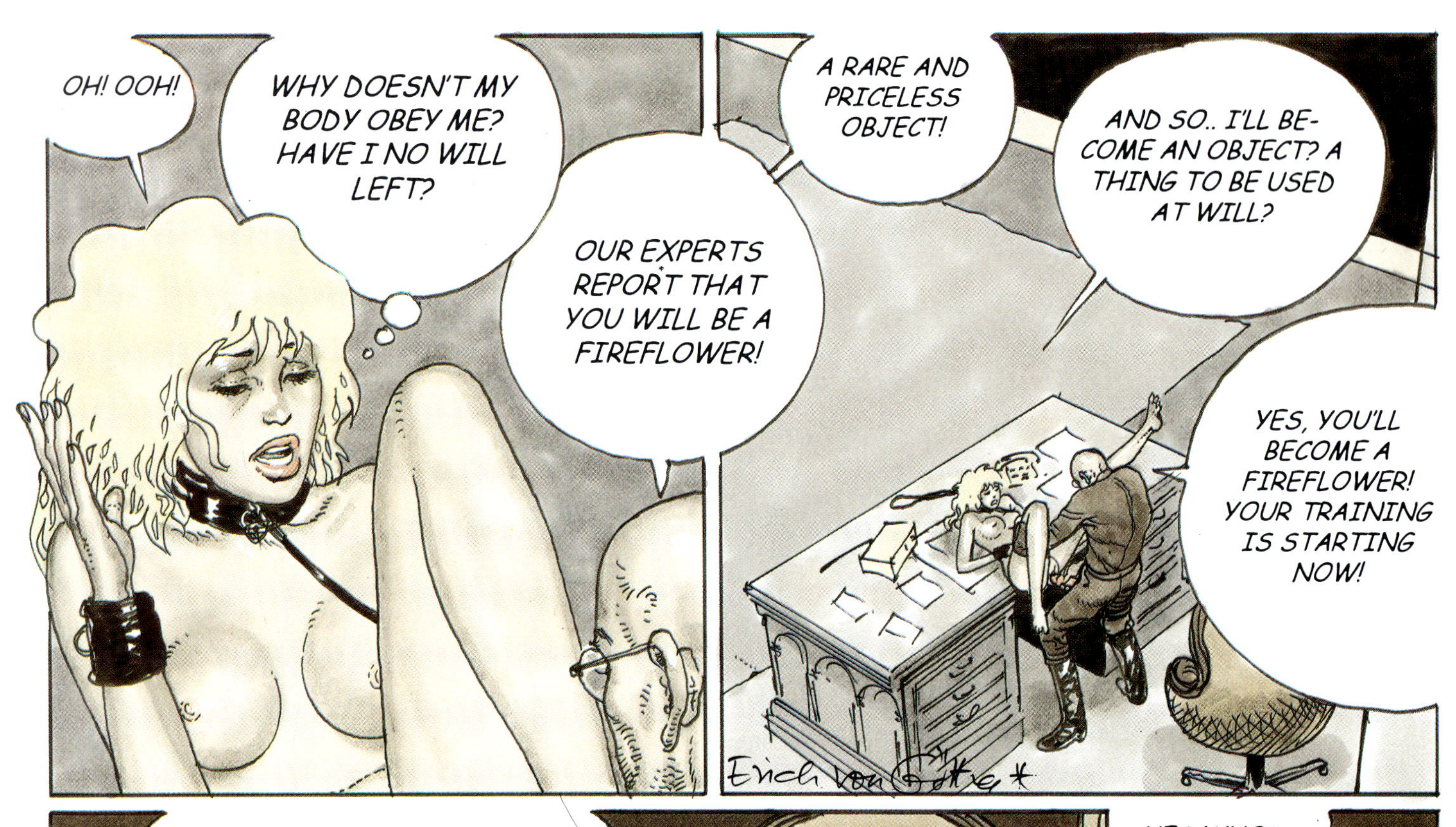
OH! OOH!
WHY DOESN'T MY BODY OBEY ME? HAVE I NO WILL LEFT?
OUR EXPERTS REPORT THAT YOU WILL BE A FIREFLOWER!
A RARE AND PRICELESS OBJECT!
AND SO.. I'LL BE-COME AN OBJECT? A THING TO BE USED AT WILL?
YES, YOU'LL BECOME A FIREFLOWER! YOUR TRAINING IS STARTING NOW!

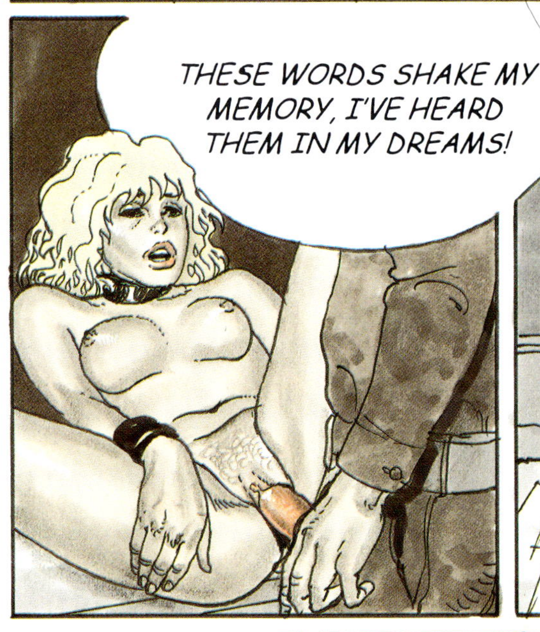
THESE WORDS SHAKE MY MEMORY, I'VE HEARD THEM IN MY DREAMS!

CAN YOU HEAR ME?
YES! AOH!

YES WHO?
AH!.. OOH!.. YES, YES MASTER!

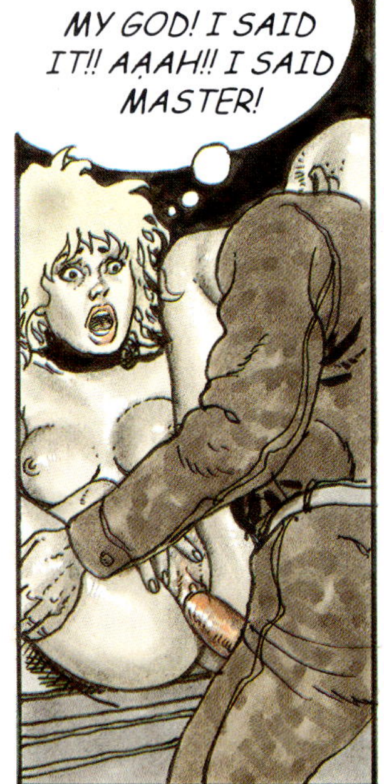
MY GOD! I SAID IT!! AAAH!! I SAID MASTER!

IS THE BITCH COMING?
AH! OH!

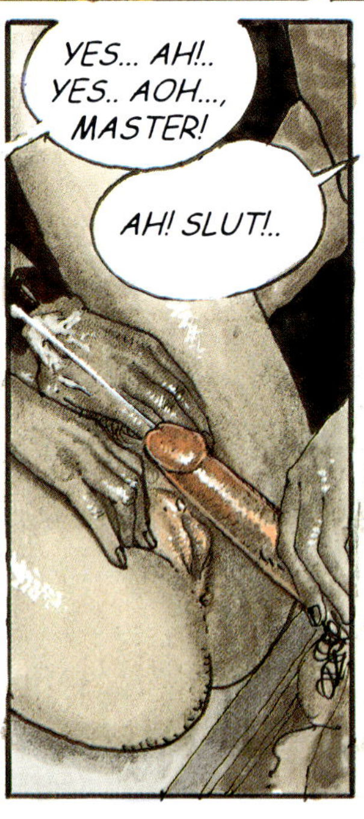
YES... AH!.. YES.. AOH..., MASTER!
AH! SLUT!..

AH! DELIGHTFUL! AND NOW... MARION! BRING IN THE SLAVES!!

HELLO, MARION, LET'S GET STARTED!
AS YOU WISH, COMMANDER! AND THIS IS MC ALISTAIR?

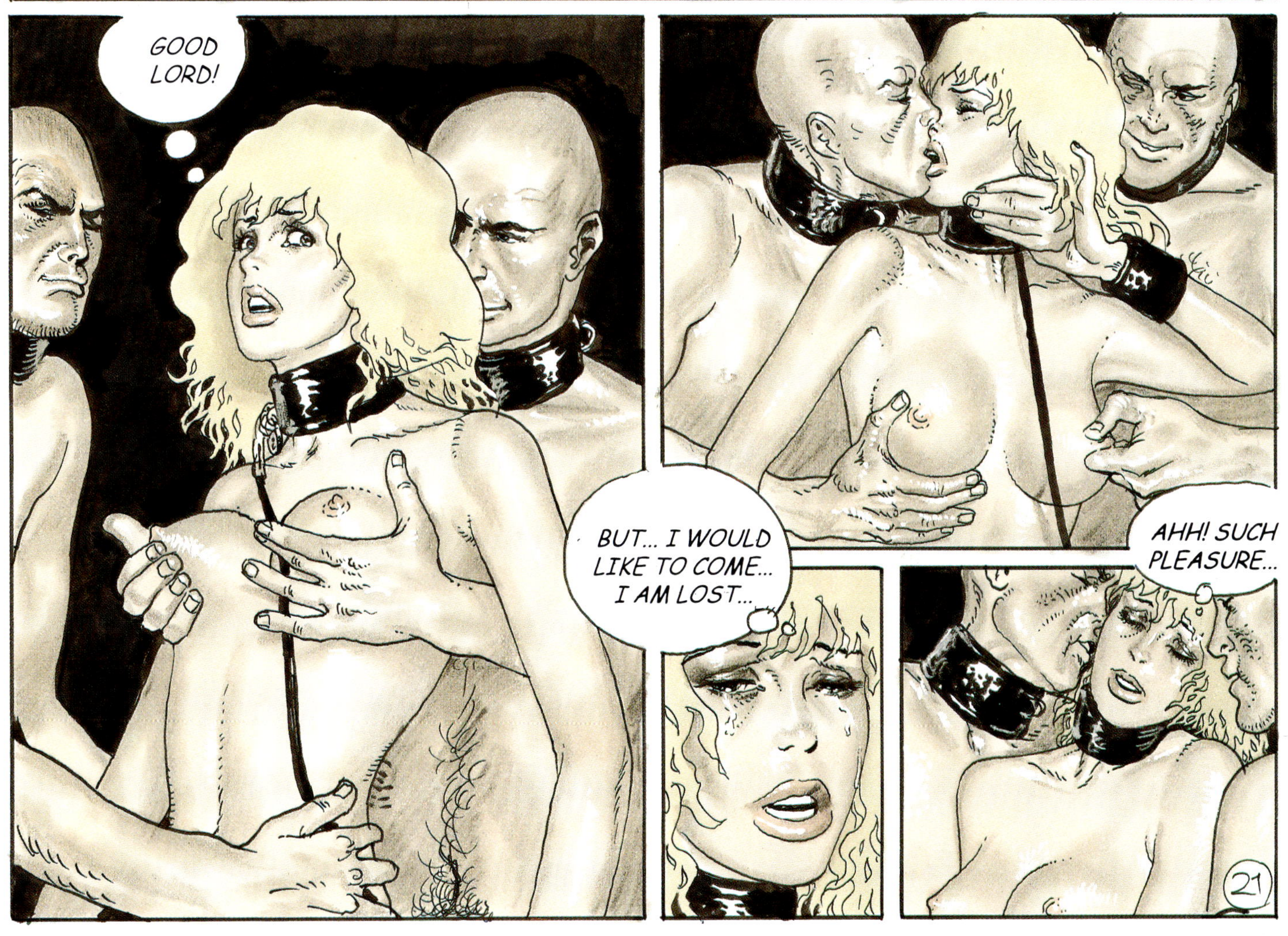
GOOD LORD!
BUT... I WOULD LIKE TO COME... I AM LOST...
AHH! SUCH PLEASURE...

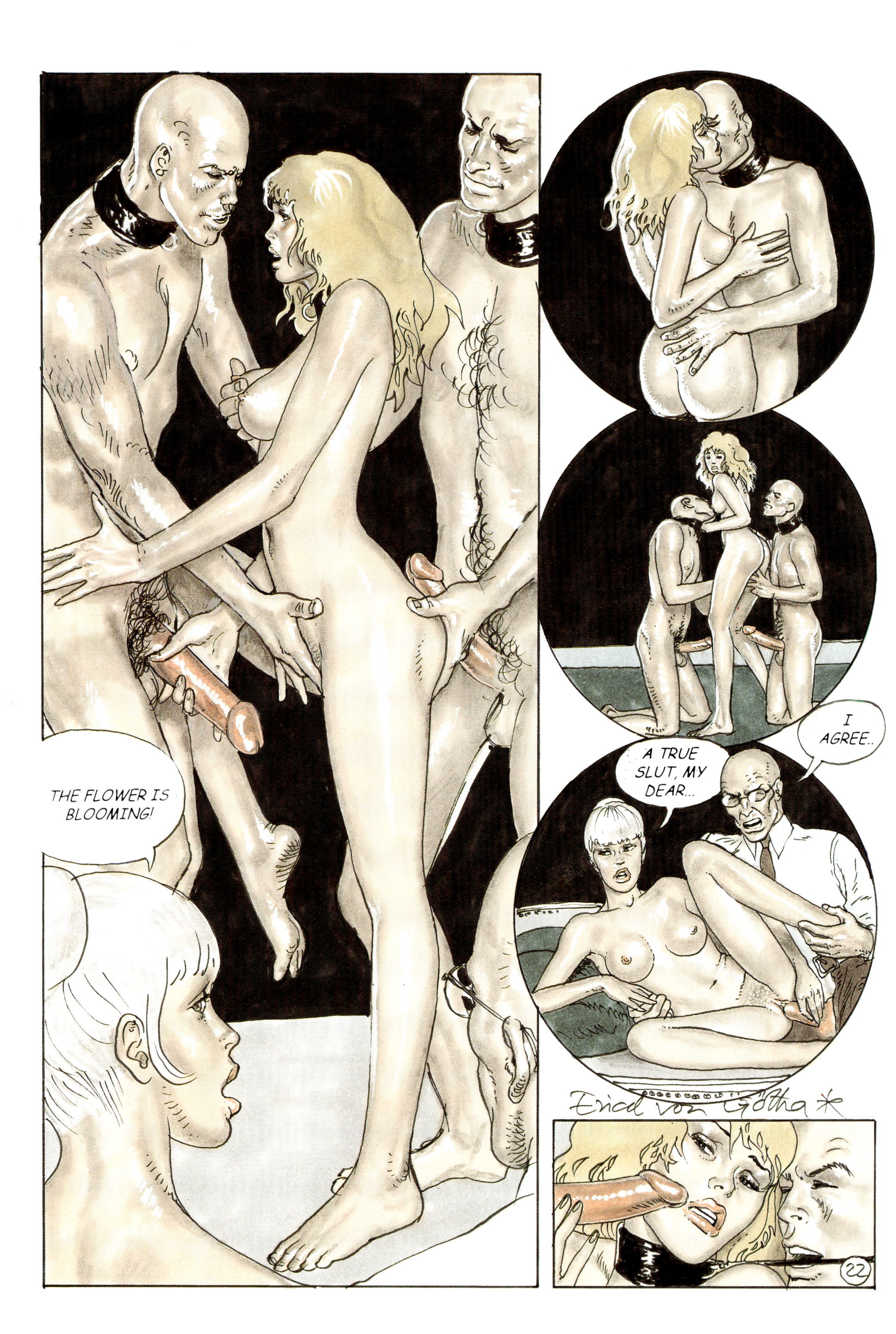
THE FLOWER IS BLOOMING!
A TRUE SLUT, MY DEAR...
I AGREE..
Erich von Götha

?...

MAYBE IT'S TRUE.. I MAY BE A TRUE SLUT...
!!!

YOU LIKE THEM TWO DICKS DON'T YOU, SLUT?
YES...
YES I LIKE TWO... OR THREE..

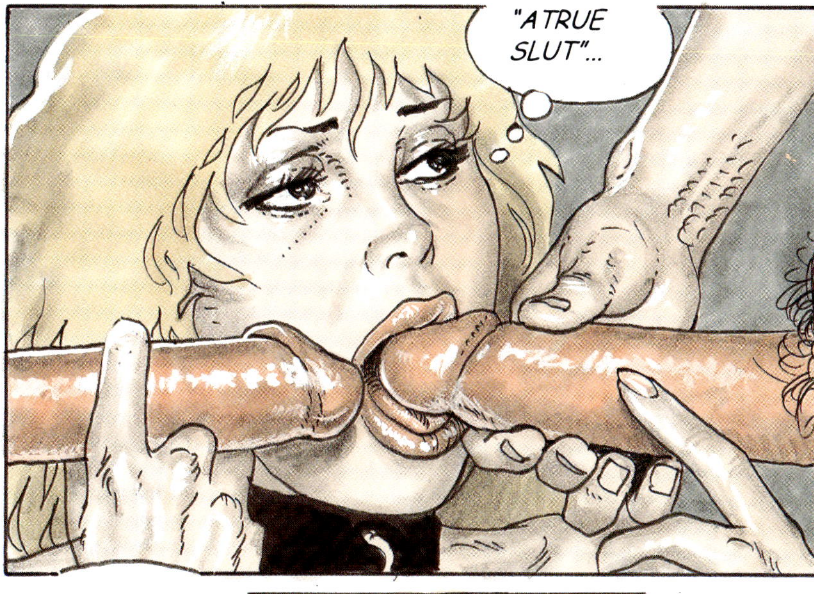
"A TRUE SLUT"...

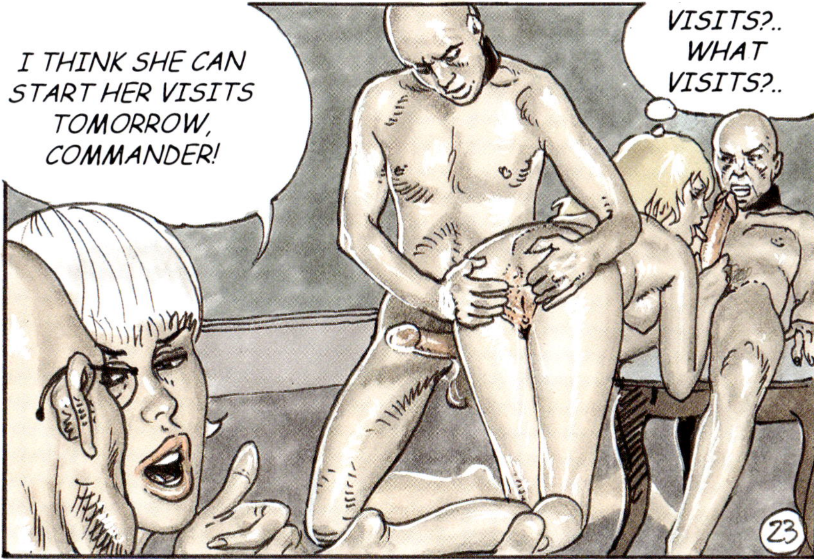
I THINK SHE CAN START HER VISITS TOMORROW, COMMANDER!
VISITS?.. WHAT VISITS?..

AAH..
OH! STICK IT IN DEEP! YOU'RE SO.. OOH! AHH!
TOMORROW, MY FRIEND?
TOMORROW, MARION!
I AM LOST... A TRUE SLUT... I LOVE SEX... I AM A... "FIRE FLOWER"!
Erich von Götha

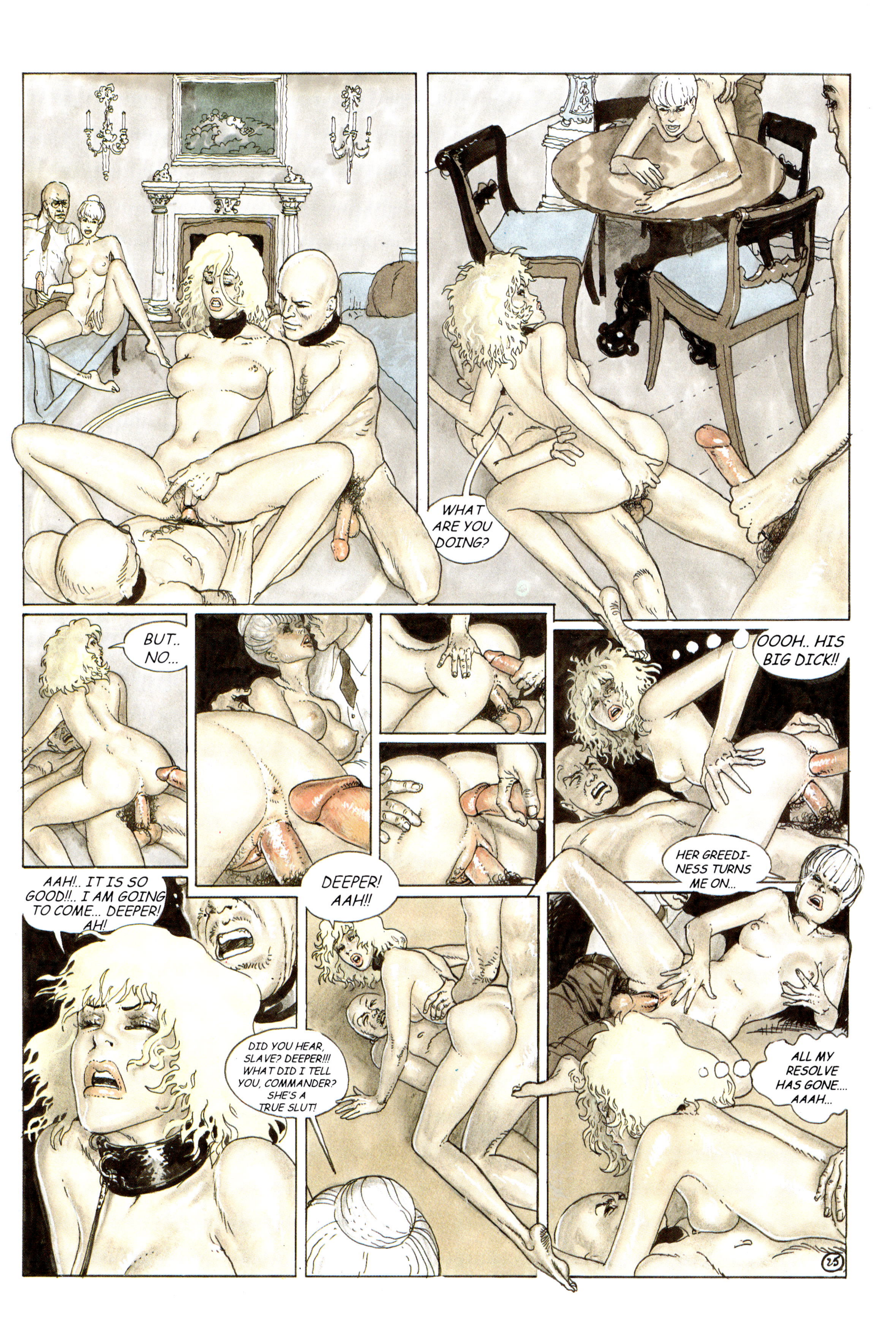
WHAT ARE YOU DOING?
BUT.. NO...
OOOH.. HIS BIG DICK!!
HER GREEDI-NESS TURNS ME ON...
AAH!.. IT IS SO GOOD!!.. I AM GOING TO COME... DEEPER! AH!
DEEPER! AAH!!
DID YOU HEAR, SLAVE? DEEPER!!! WHAT DID I TELL YOU, COMMANDER? SHE'S A TRUE SLUT!
ALL MY RESOLVE HAS GONE.... AAAH...

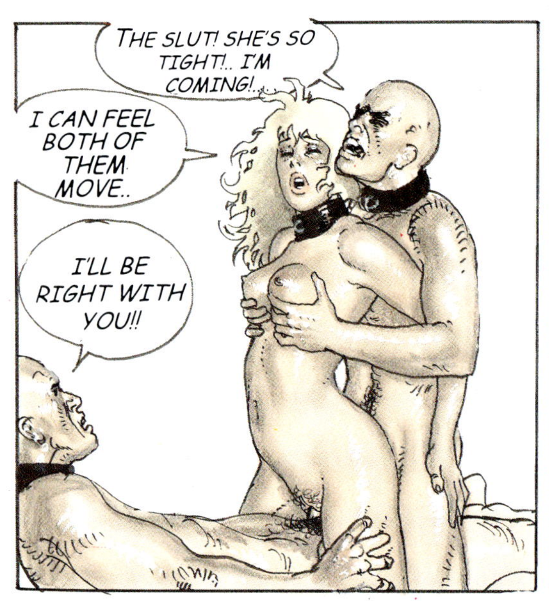
THE SLUT! SHE'S SO TIGHT!.. I'M COMING!..
I CAN FEEL BOTH OF THEM MOVE..
I'LL BE RIGHT WITH YOU!!

UNBELIEV-ABLE LAY! AAAH!!
LOOK! SHE'S FAINTED!

AM I HOME? BUT.. NO.. I'M STILL HERE, WHERE I CAN BE ANYBODY'S EASY PREY, THE DEFENSELESS VICTIM OF THEIR CYNICAL GAMES.. SO..
WHY DO I LIKE IT SO MUCH?

GET UP! YOU'RE LEAVING!

GET DRESSED! IMMEDI-ATELY!
LEAVE? WHERE TO?

WHERE ARE YOU TAKING ME? WILL I BE FREED?
YOU'RE LUCKY, SLUT! YOUR CASE HAS BEEN REVIEWED...

YOU MEAN I HAVE TO GO TO COURT AGAIN?
THE CASE HAS SOME.. IRREGU-LARITIES...
GET OUT OF HERE!
NO COLLAR?!
NO CHAINS?!
IS IT TRUE? AM I REALLY FREE OF THIS SORDID ESTAB-LISHMENT?
THEY DON'T LOOK LIKE GUARDS... THEY ARE REAL COPS...
PLEASE, CLIMB IN .. WE'RE GOING TO BE LATE..
MAYBE I CAN TELL THEM MY STORY...
..OR MAYBE I SHOULD WAIT!..
LOOK!
WHAT IS...?
REMOVALS
WHAT DO YOU WANT?
HERE! THE KEYS!
HELP?! DY MY FIANCE SEND YOU?
YES MISS, RIGHT! YOUR FIANCE HIM-SELF!

SO HE DID NOT FORGET ME...?
NO WAY, DOLL! HE PAID US TO GET YOU OUT..
GET IN NOW!.. WE'RE IN A RUSH!
A CHILD'S GAME. WE WRECKED THEIR RADIO BEFORE LEAVING. THEY SURRENDERED!
THANK YOU FOR TAKING SO MUCH RISK FOR ME.. I'LL BE GRATEFUL..
ALSO I.. HE..
HOW GRATE-FUL CAN YOU GET?...
GOOD LORD!
DICKHEADS! WHY DO YOU MAKE A MESS OF IT? PETER...
KLIK!
...WILL HAVE YOU SHOT FOR THIS! LET ME GO NOW!
SHUT UP!
HERE WE ARE.. TOO BAD.. IT LOOKS LIKE YOU REALLY LIKE TO FUCK! DON'T YOU THINK, HARRY?
AH... NO.. HAVE MERCY.. PLEASE... I CAN'T... AAAH!..
IT SEEMS THERE'S NO OTHER CHOICE FOR EMMA.. EVEN WHEN I'M SAVED... YET, IT TURNS ME ON...
!!!
SHE'S WETTER THAN SEATTLE.. TOO BAD WE CAN'T KEEP HER A DAY OR TWO...

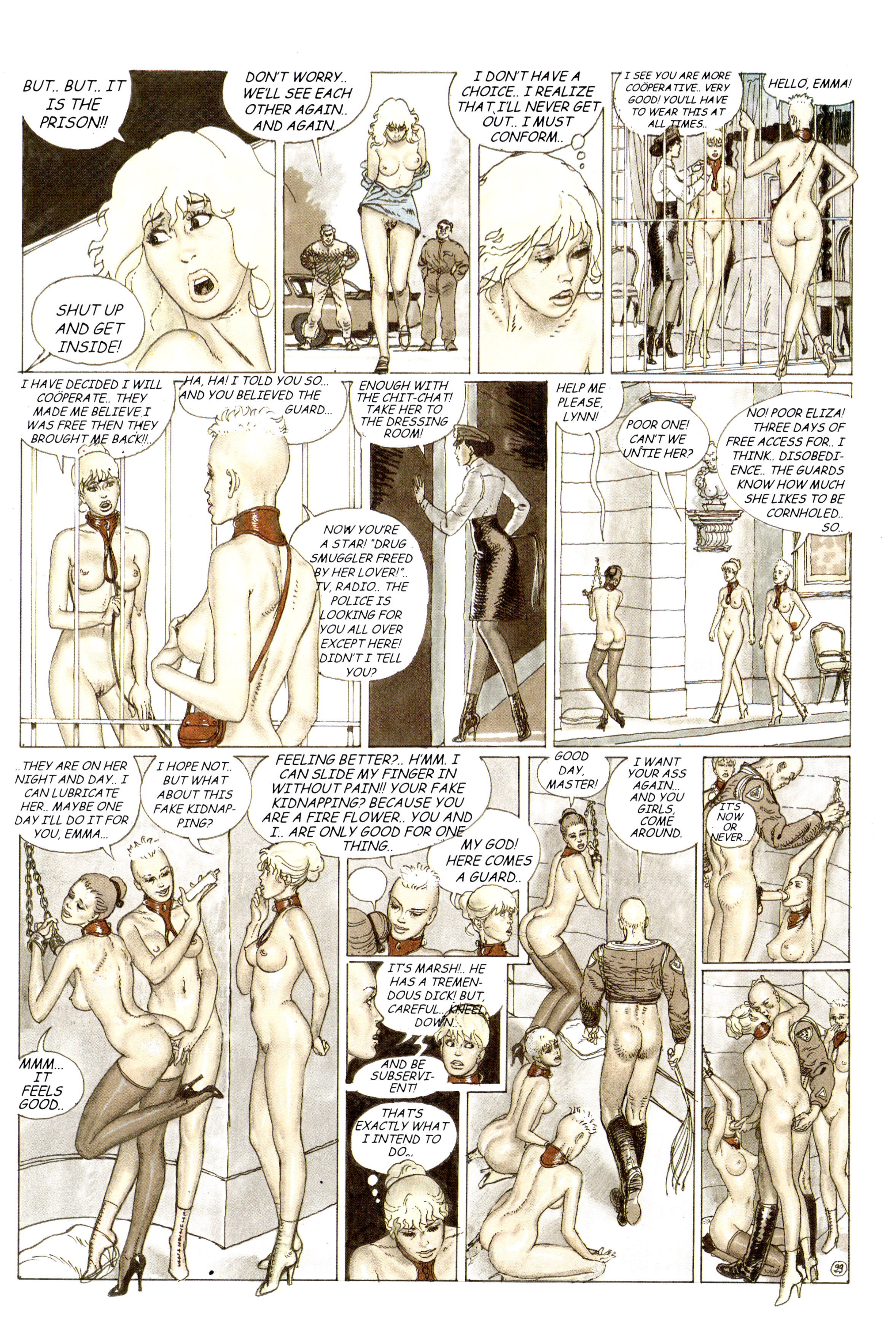
BUT.. BUT.. IT IS THE PRISON!!
SHUT UP AND GET INSIDE!
DON'T WORRY.. WE'LL SEE EACH OTHER AGAIN.. AND AGAIN..
I DON'T HAVE A CHOICE.. I REALIZE THAT I'LL NEVER GET OUT.. I MUST CONFORM..
I SEE YOU ARE MORE COÖPERATIVE.. VERY GOOD! YOU'LL HAVE TO WEAR THIS AT ALL TIMES..
HELLO, EMMA!
I HAVE DECIDED I WILL COÖPERATE.. THEY MADE ME BELIEVE I WAS FREE THEN THEY BROUGHT ME BACK!!..
HA, HA! I TOLD YOU SO... AND YOU BELIEVED THE GUARD...
NOW YOU'RE A STAR! "DRUG SMUGGLER FREED BY HER LOVER!".. TV, RADIO.. THE POLICE IS LOOKING FOR YOU ALL OVER EXCEPT HERE! DIDN'T I TELL YOU?
ENOUGH WITH THE CHIT-CHAT! TAKE HER TO THE DRESSING ROOM!
HELP ME PLEASE, LYNN!
POOR ONE! CAN'T WE UNTIE HER?
NO! POOR ELIZA! THREE DAYS OF FREE ACCESS FOR.. I THINK.. DISOBEDIENCE.. THE GUARDS KNOW HOW MUCH SHE LIKES TO BE CORNHOLED.. SO..
..THEY ARE ON HER NIGHT AND DAY.. I CAN LUBRICATE HER.. MAYBE ONE DAY I'LL DO IT FOR YOU, EMMA...
I HOPE NOT.. BUT WHAT ABOUT THIS FAKE KIDNAPPING?
MMM... IT FEELS GOOD..
FEELING BETTER?.. H'MM. I CAN SLIDE MY FINGER IN WITHOUT PAIN!! YOUR FAKE KIDNAPPING? BECAUSE YOU ARE A FIRE FLOWER.. YOU AND I.. ARE ONLY GOOD FOR ONE THING..
MY GOD! HERE COMES A GUARD..
IT'S MARSH!.. HE HAS A TREMENDOUS DICK! BUT, CAREFUL.. KNEEL DOWN..
AND BE SUBSERVIENT!
THAT'S EXACTLY WHAT I INTEND TO DO..
GOOD DAY, MASTER!
I WANT YOUR ASS AGAIN.. AND YOU GIRLS, COME AROUND.
IT'S NOW OR NEVER...

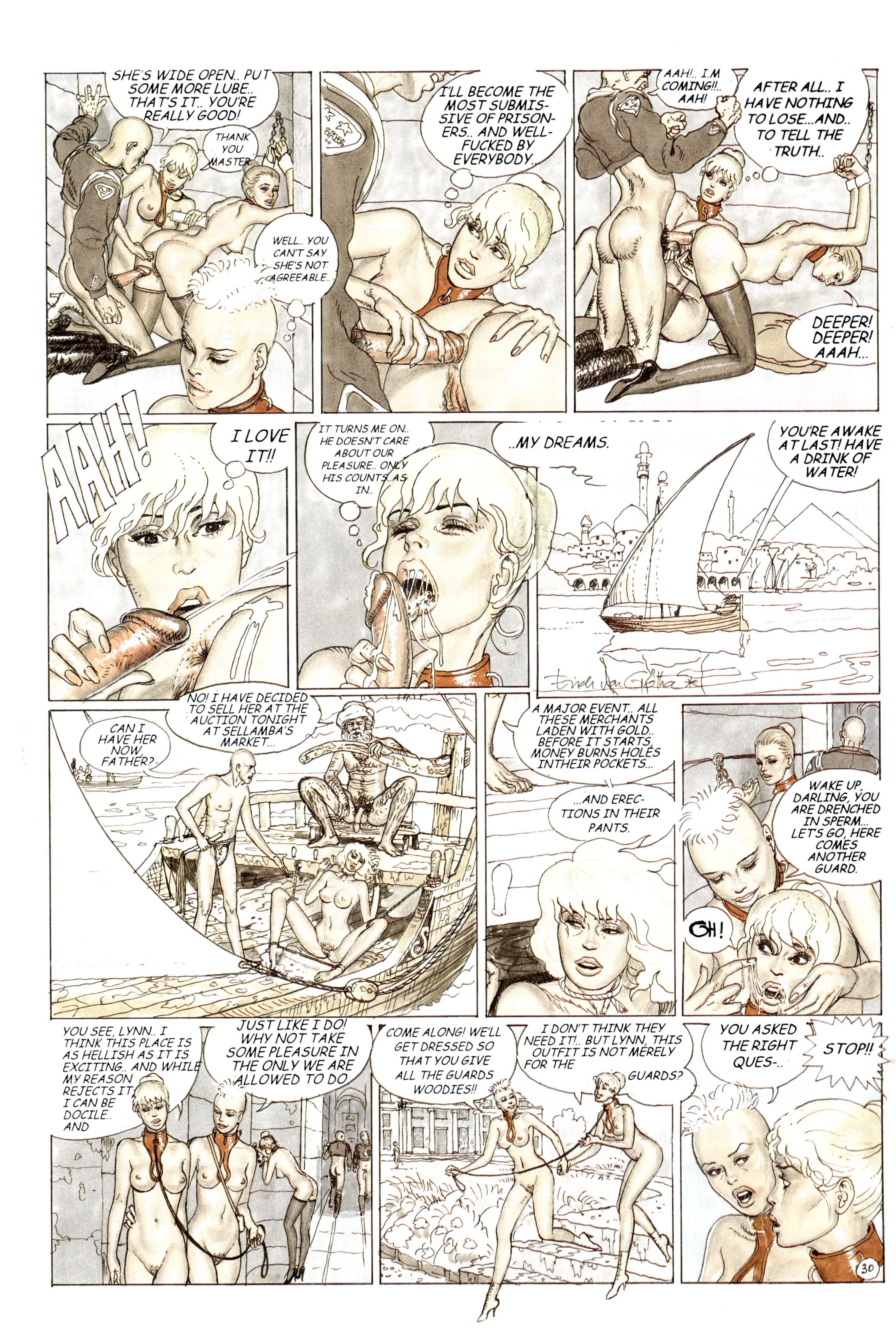

SHE'S WIDE OPEN.. PUT SOME MORE LUBE.. THAT'S IT.. YOU'RE REALLY GOOD!
THANK YOU MASTER
WELL.. YOU CAN'T SAY SHE'S NOT AGREEABLE..
I'LL BECOME THE MOST SUBMISSIVE OF PRISONERS.. AND WELL-FUCKED BY EVERYBODY...
AAH!.. I.M COMING!!.. AAH!
AFTER ALL.. I HAVE NOTHING TO LOSE...AND.. TO TELL THE TRUTH..
DEEPER! DEEPER! AAAH...
AAH!
I LOVE IT!!
IT TURNS ME ON.. HE DOESN'T CARE ABOUT OUR PLEASURE.. ONLY HIS COUNTS..AS IN..
..MY DREAMS.
YOU'RE AWAKE AT LAST! HAVE A DRINK OF WATER!
CAN I HAVE HER NOW, FATHER?
NO! I HAVE DECIDED TO SELL HER AT THE AUCTION TONIGHT AT SELLAMBA'S MARKET...
A MAJOR EVENT.. ALL THESE MERCHANTS LADEN WITH GOLD.. BEFORE IT STARTS, MONEY BURNS HOLES INTHEIR POCKETS...
...AND ERECTIONS IN THEIR PANTS.
WAKE UP, DARLING, YOU ARE DRENCHED IN SPERM... LET'S GO, HERE COMES ANOTHER GUARD.
OH!
YOU SEE, LYNN.. I THINK THIS PLACE IS AS HELLISH AS IT IS EXCITING.. AND WHILE MY REASON REJECTS IT, I CAN BE DOCILE.. AND
JUST LIKE I DO! WHY NOT TAKE SOME PLEASURE IN THE ONLY WE ARE ALLOWED TO DO
COME ALONG! WE'LL GET DRESSED SO THAT YOU GIVE ALL THE GUARDS WOODIES!!
I DON'T THINK THEY NEED IT!.. BUT LYNN, THIS OUTFIT IS NOT MERELY FOR THE GUARDS?
YOU ASKED THE RIGHT QUES-..
STOP!!

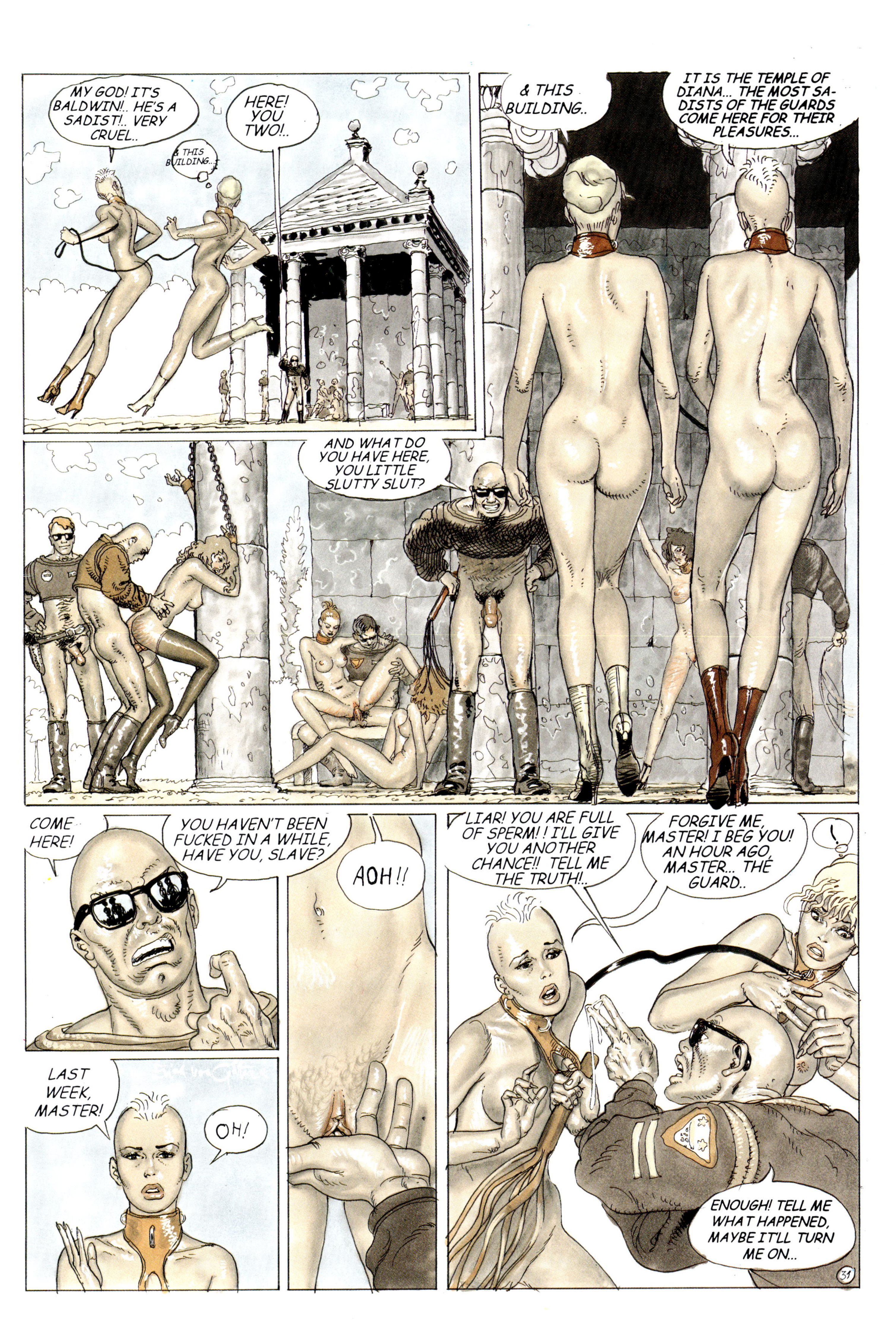
MY GOD! IT'S BALDWIN!.. HE'S A SADIST!.. VERY CRUEL..
& THIS BUILDING..
HERE! YOU TWO!..
& THIS BUILDING..
IT IS THE TEMPLE OF DIANA... THE MOST SADISTS OF THE GUARDS COME HERE FOR THEIR PLEASURES...
AND WHAT DO YOU HAVE HERE, YOU LITTLE SLUTTY SLUT?
COME HERE!
YOU HAVEN'T BEEN FUCKED IN A WHILE, HAVE YOU, SLAVE?
AOH!!
LAST WEEK, MASTER!
OH!
LIAR! YOU ARE FULL OF SPERM!! I'LL GIVE YOU ANOTHER CHANCE!! TELL ME THE TRUTH!..
FORGIVE ME, MASTER! I BEG YOU! AN HOUR AGO, MASTER... THE GUARD..
!
ENOUGH! TELL ME WHAT HAPPENED, MAYBE IT'LL TURN ME ON...

I WAS ON MY WAY TO MEET THIS UNASSIGNED FIREFLOWER.. I MET A GUARD.. HE WANTED TO KNOW WHERE... THEN HIS IDEA CHANGED, HE TIED ME UP...

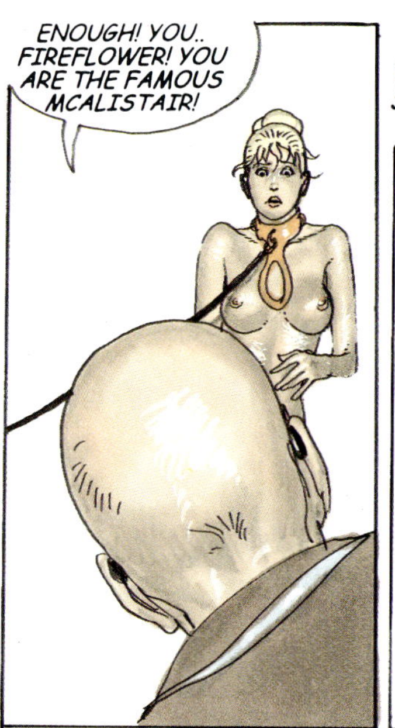
ENOUGH! YOU.. FIREFLOWER! YOU ARE THE FAMOUS MCALISTAIR!

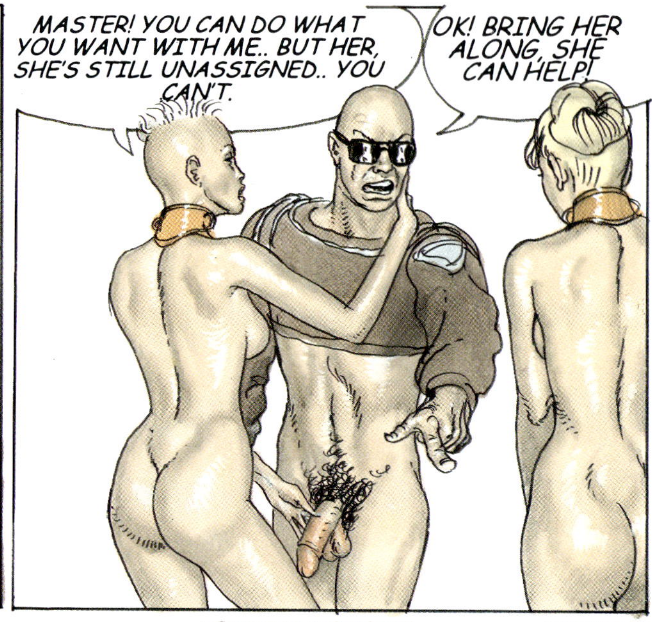
MASTER! YOU CAN DO WHAT YOU WANT WITH ME.. BUT HER, SHE'S STILL UNASSIGNED.. YOU CAN'T.
OK! BRING HER ALONG, SHE CAN HELP!

I TOLD YOU... A TEMPLE OF SADISTS...

GOOD!.. AND NOW LET'S FUCK!

AND YOU, WHEN YOU ARE ASSIGNED, I'LL FUCK YOU TOO!

SLUT! OPEN HER FOR ME!
HMMMM
Erich von Götha

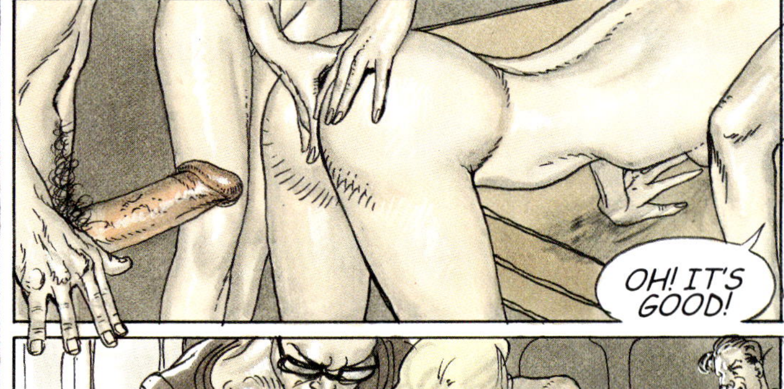
OH! IT'S GOOD!

YES! FUCK ME, MASTER!

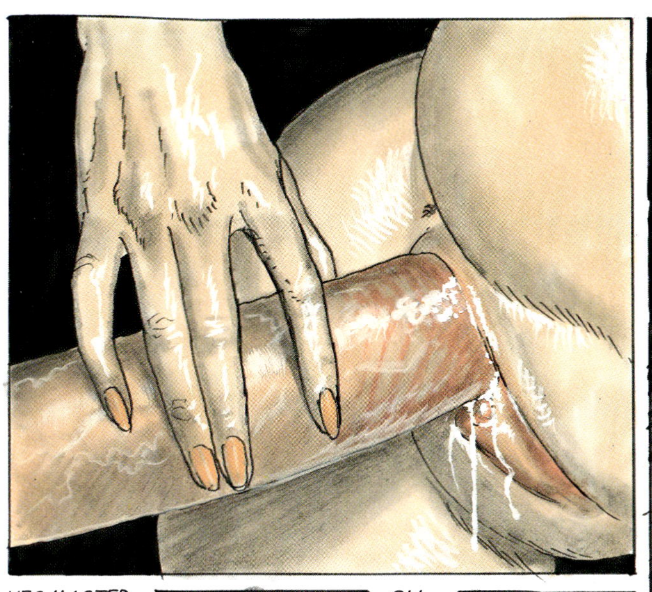

OH! YES!..
OH!..

HMMMM! ..SEEMS LIKE YOUR NEW LITTLE RECRUIT ENJOYS THIS, DOESN'T SHE?

YES MASTER, SHE'S JUST CRAZY ABOUT IT, BUT...
OH, BUT...

SHE'LL BE SOLD TO A WHOREHOUSE? OR A BILLIONAIRE? OR A POP STAR? OR AN EMIR? OR A SADIST FROM THE MIDDLE EAST?
SOLD?.. ME...

AAH!.. AOH!.. MM.. I DON'T KNOW, MAS-TER.. MOST FIREFLOWERS ARE SOLD MANY TIMES. MYSELF, I HAVE..
FIRE FLOWER?

THAT'S HOW...AOHH... SHE HAS BEEN CLASSIFIED... AAAH... MM.
A NEW FIREFLOWER! WHAT LUCK! I WANT HER!!
FORGIVE ME MASTER.. BUT... YOU'RE RISK-ING CAPITAL PUNISHMENT... AAH..

MMMM.. SPREAD YOUR LEGS.. I WANT HER.. AND.. WHO WOULD TELL ON ME?
YEAH.. YEAH.. STICK IT IN.. FILL ME UP!...
ME!!

GOOD LORD!

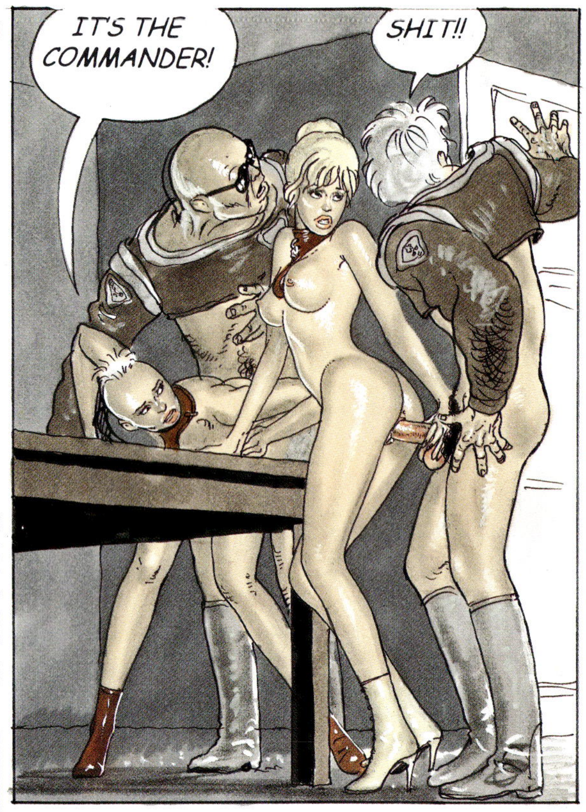
IT'S THE COMMANDER!
SHIT!!

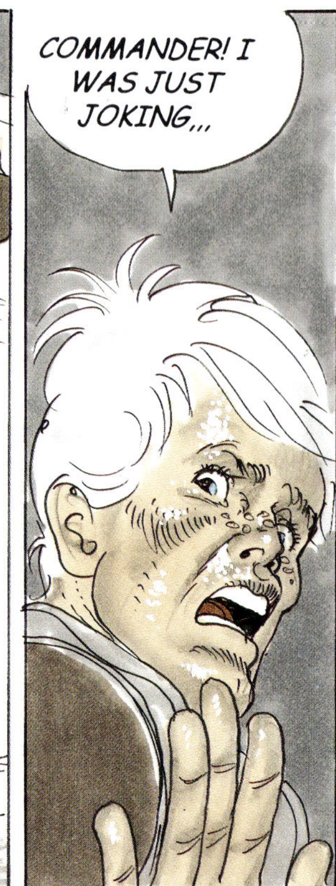
COMMANDER! I WAS JUST JOKING,,,

TOO LATE, SON.. THE SLAVE WAS RIGHT!..SUCH DELIBER-ATE DISOBEDIENCE IS CAUSE FOR INSTANT TERMINATION!

NO! NO! I, I, ...

MKLGH..

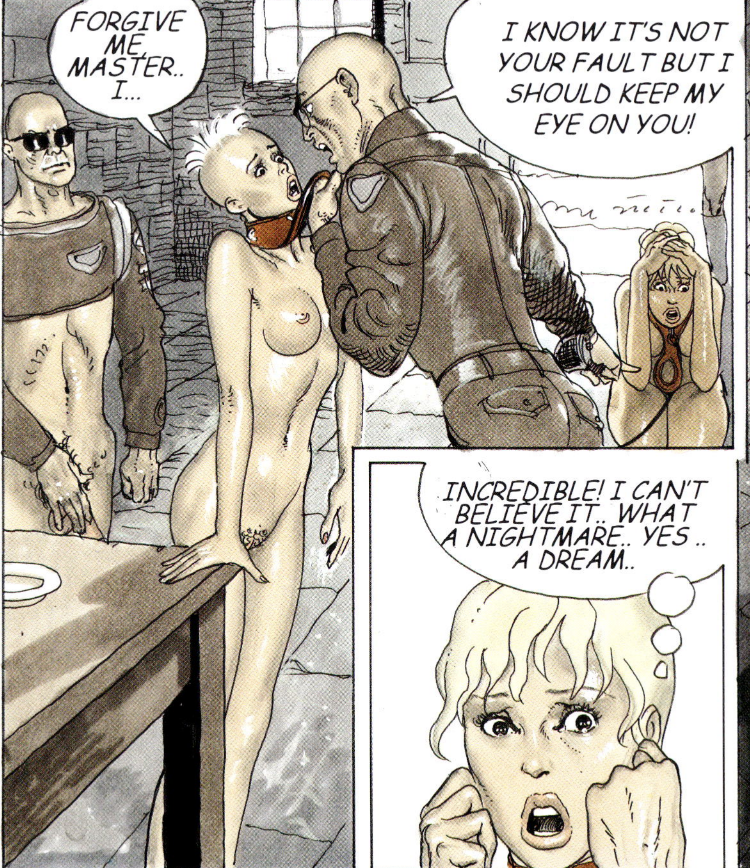
FORGIVE ME MASTER.. I...
I KNOW IT'S NOT YOUR FAULT BUT I SHOULD KEEP MY EYE ON YOU!
INCREDIBLE! I CAN'T BELIEVE IT.. WHAT A NIGHTMARE.. YES .. A DREAM..

GUARD! TAKE THIS GARBAGE AWAY! HAVE HIS NAME DELETED FROM THE RECORDS!
HOR-RIBLE!

ANY MISTAKE CAN BE LETHAL HERE, EMMA! SECURITY NEEDS.. YOU ARE LUCKY YOU HAVE BEEN GIVEN A CHANCE TO LIVE AFTER WHAT YOU DID...
LUCKY?..

LUCKY TO NOT BE RAPED 10 TIMES A DAY? LUCKY TO NOT BE EXECUTED? OR LUCKY TO HAVE BEEN TORN AWAY FROM MY LIFE, MY FRIENDS, MY FAMILY, MY HOUSE?

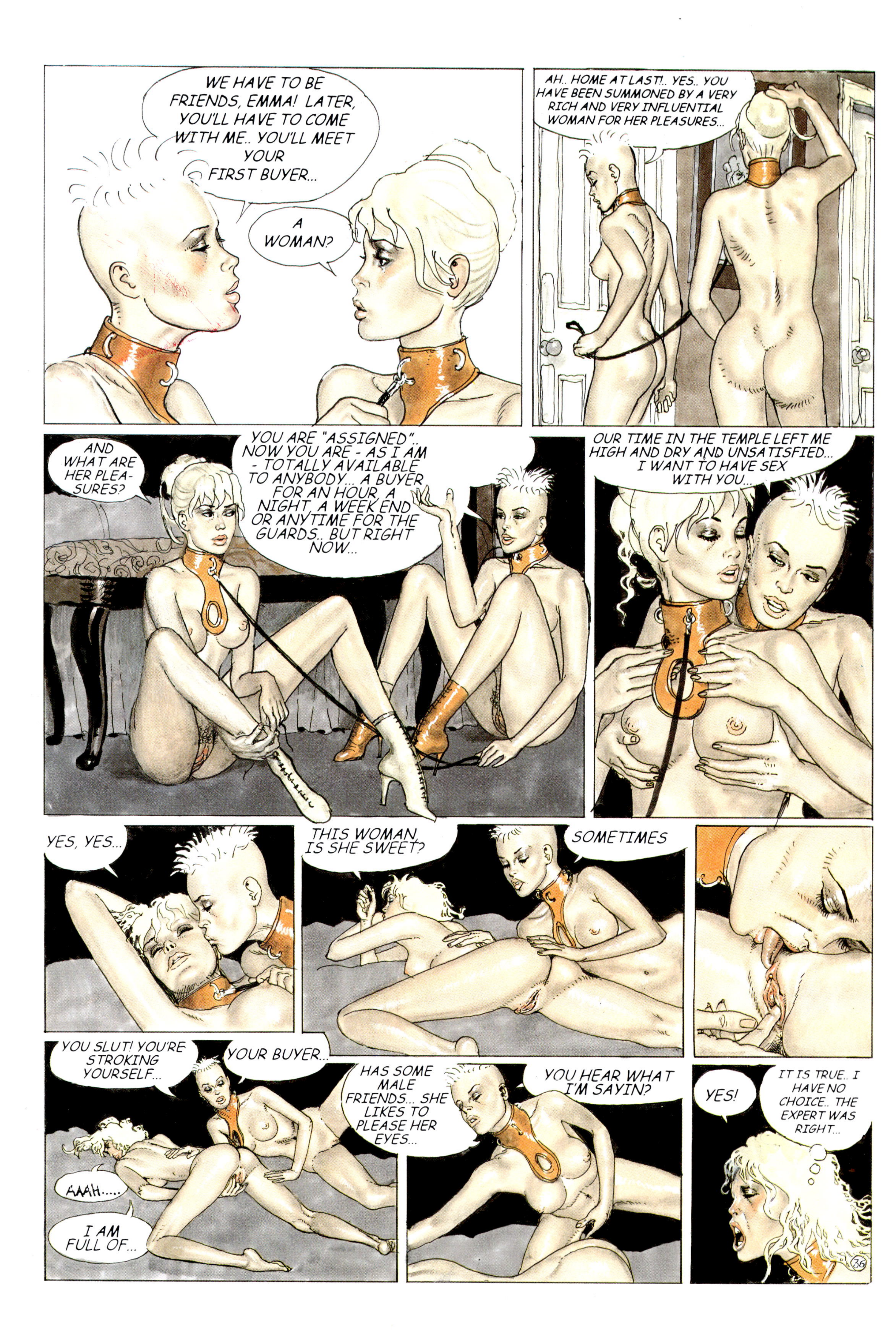
WE HAVE TO BE FRIENDS, EMMA! LATER, YOU'LL HAVE TO COME WITH ME.. YOU'LL MEET YOUR FIRST BUYER...
A WOMAN?
AH.. HOME AT LAST!.. YES.. YOU HAVE BEEN SUMMONED BY A VERY RICH AND VERY INFLUENTIAL WOMAN FOR HER PLEASURES...
AND WHAT ARE HER PLEASURES?
YOU ARE "ASSIGNED".. NOW YOU ARE - AS I AM - TOTALLY AVAILABLE TO ANYBODY... A BUYER FOR AN HOUR, A NIGHT, A WEEK END OR ANYTIME FOR THE GUARDS.. BUT RIGHT NOW...
OUR TIME IN THE TEMPLE LEFT ME HIGH AND DRY AND UNSATISFIED... I WANT TO HAVE SEX WITH YOU...
YES, YES...
THIS WOMAN, IS SHE SWEET?
SOMETIMES
YOU SLUT! YOU'RE STROKING YOURSELF...
YOUR BUYER...
AAAH.....
I AM FULL OF...
HAS SOME MALE FRIENDS... SHE LIKES TO PLEASE HER EYES...
YOU HEAR WHAT I'M SAYIN?
YES!
IT IS TRUE.. I HAVE NO CHOICE.. THE EXPERT WAS RIGHT...
36

Erich von Götha

LET'S GO SLAVES!!
AOH!
YES MASTER!!
GO SEE THE COMMANDER RIGHT AWAY!!

IS SHE THE NEW FIRE FLOWER?
YES, MASTER
IS SHE STILL ASSIGNED?
YES, TONIGHT MASTER..
READY TO FUCK..

VERY GOOD..
BRING HER NEAR THE WINDOW... I WANT TO LOOK AT HER... MMM.. CUTE.. COME CLOSER SLUT..!

TAKE MY DICK AND SUCK IT, BITCH!
YES, MASTER...

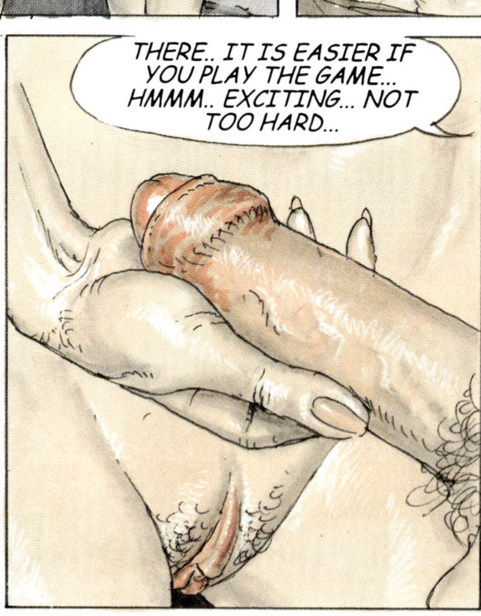
THERE.. IT IS EASIER IF YOU PLAY THE GAME... HMMM.. EXCITING... NOT TOO HARD...

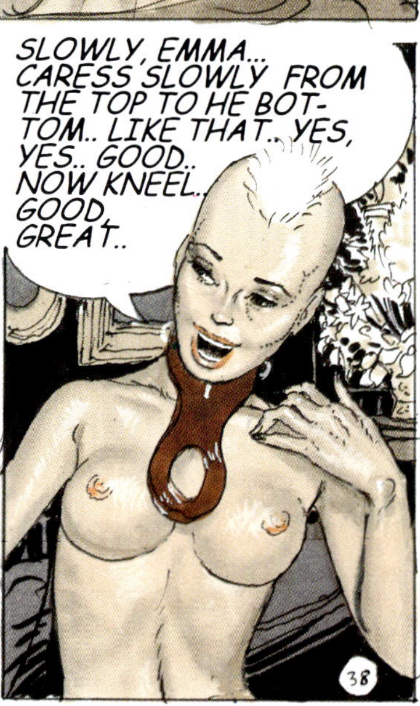
SLOWLY, EMMA... CARESS SLOWLY FROM THE TOP TO HE BOTTOM.. LIKE THAT.. YES, YES.. GOOD.. NOW KNEEL.. GOOD, GREAT..

HOLD HIS BALLS.. AND LET THE TIP OF HIS DICK ENTER YOUR LIPS.. YES.. HMMM..
HMM.. AAH..
MMN..

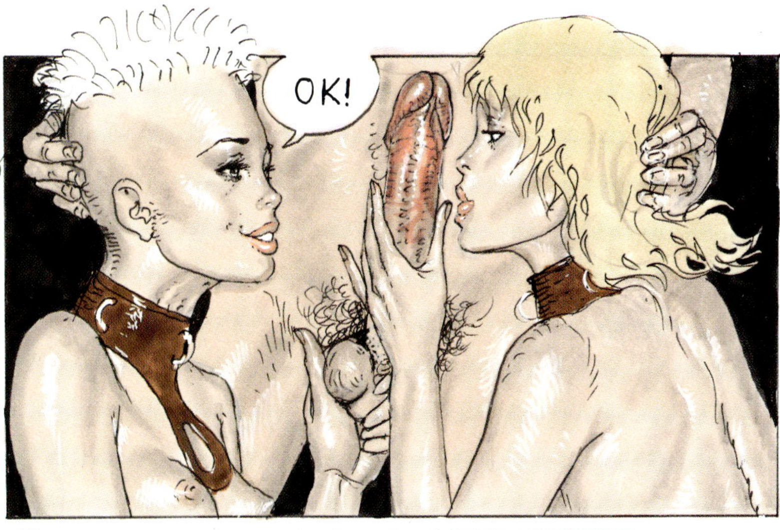
OK!

NOT BAD...

A REAL SLUT.. MM..

WITH MORE THAN JUST A PRETTY FACE!

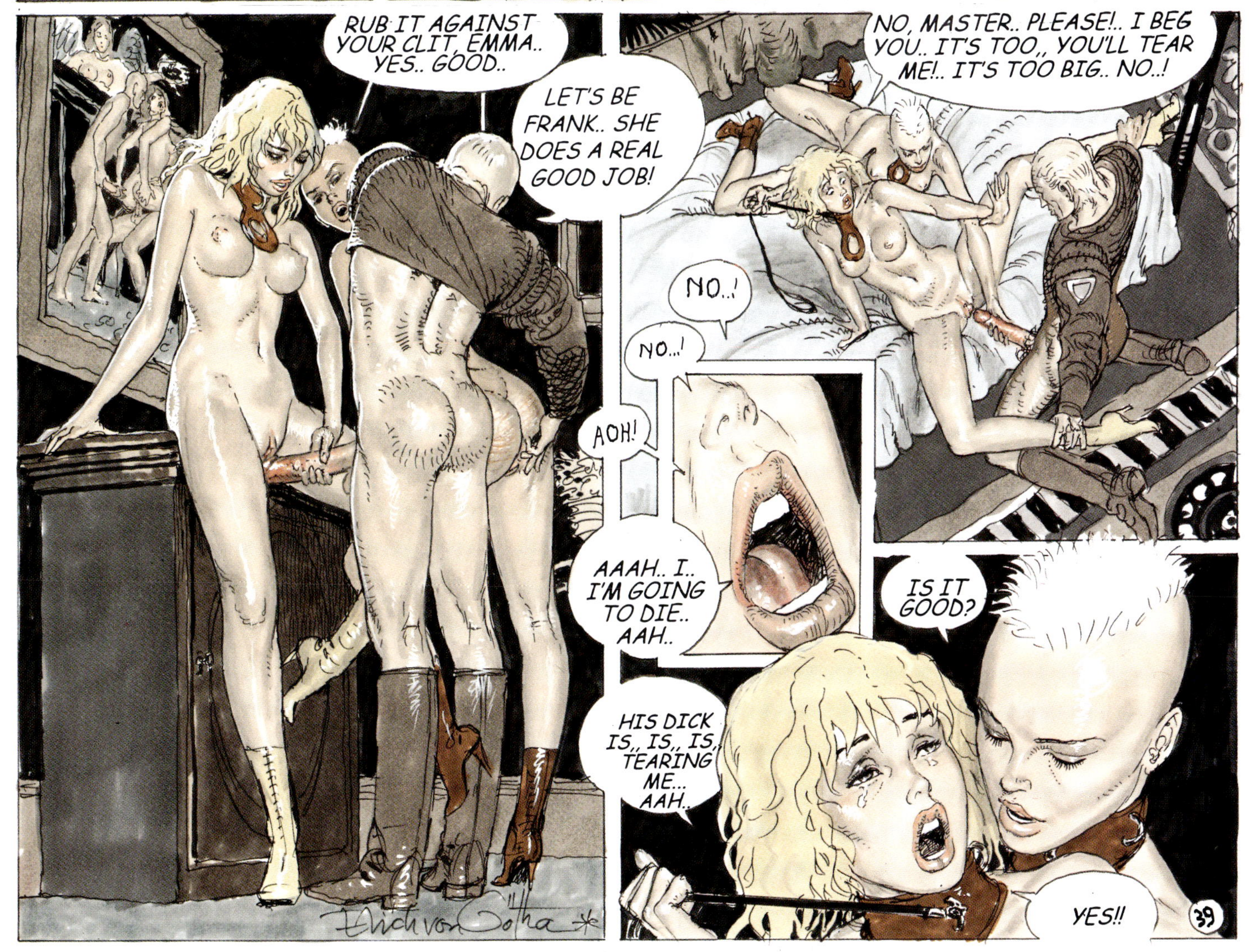
RUB IT AGAINST YOUR CLIT, EMMA.. YES.. GOOD..
LET'S BE FRANK.. SHE DOES A REAL GOOD JOB!
NO, MASTER.. PLEASE!.. I BEG YOU.. IT'S TOO,, YOU'LL TEAR ME!.. IT'S TOO BIG.. NO..!
NO..!
NO..!
AOH!
AAAH.. I.. I'M GOING TO DIE.. AAH..
IS IT GOOD?
HIS DICK IS,, IS,, IS, TEARING ME... AAH..
YES!!

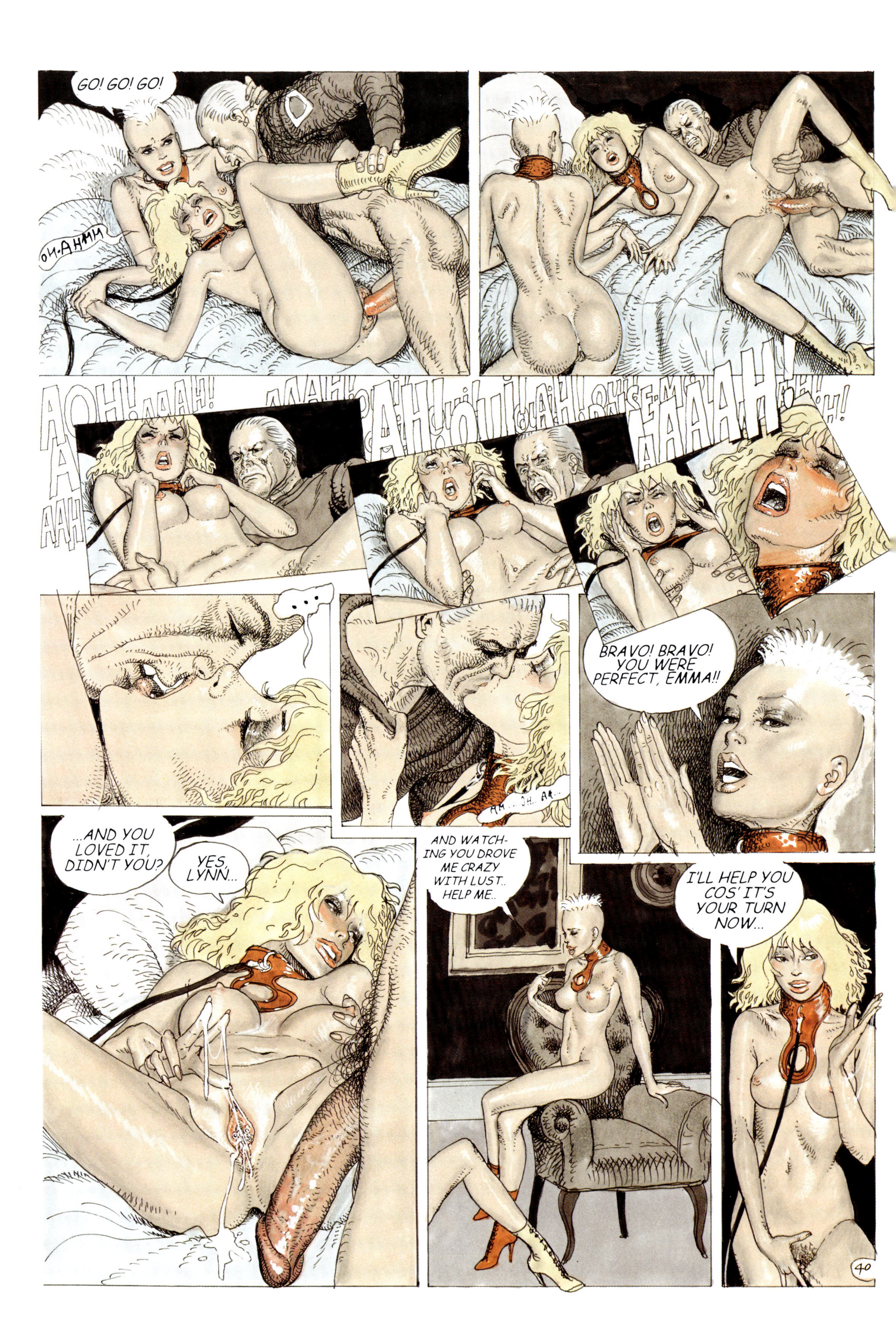
GO! GO! GO!
OH-AHMM
AOH! AAAH!
AAAH!
AH!
OUI!
AAAAH!
...
AH... OH... AH...
BRAVO! BRAVO! YOU WERE PERFECT, EMMA!!
...AND YOU LOVED IT, DIDN'T YOU?
YES, LYNN...
AND WATCHING YOU DROVE ME CRAZY WITH LUST.. HELP ME..
I'LL HELP YOU COS' IT'S YOUR TURN NOW...

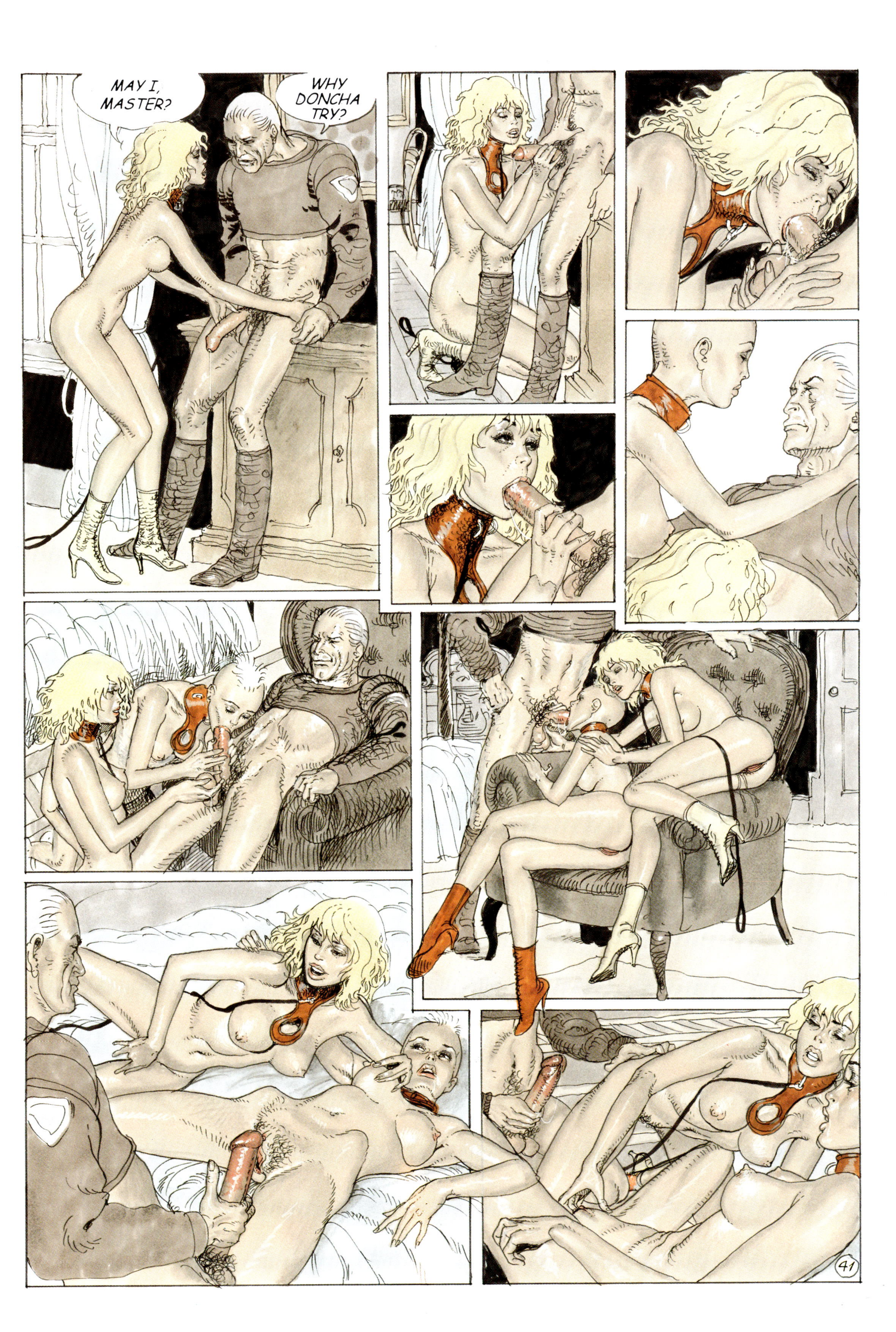
MAY I, MASTER?
WHY DONCHA TRY?

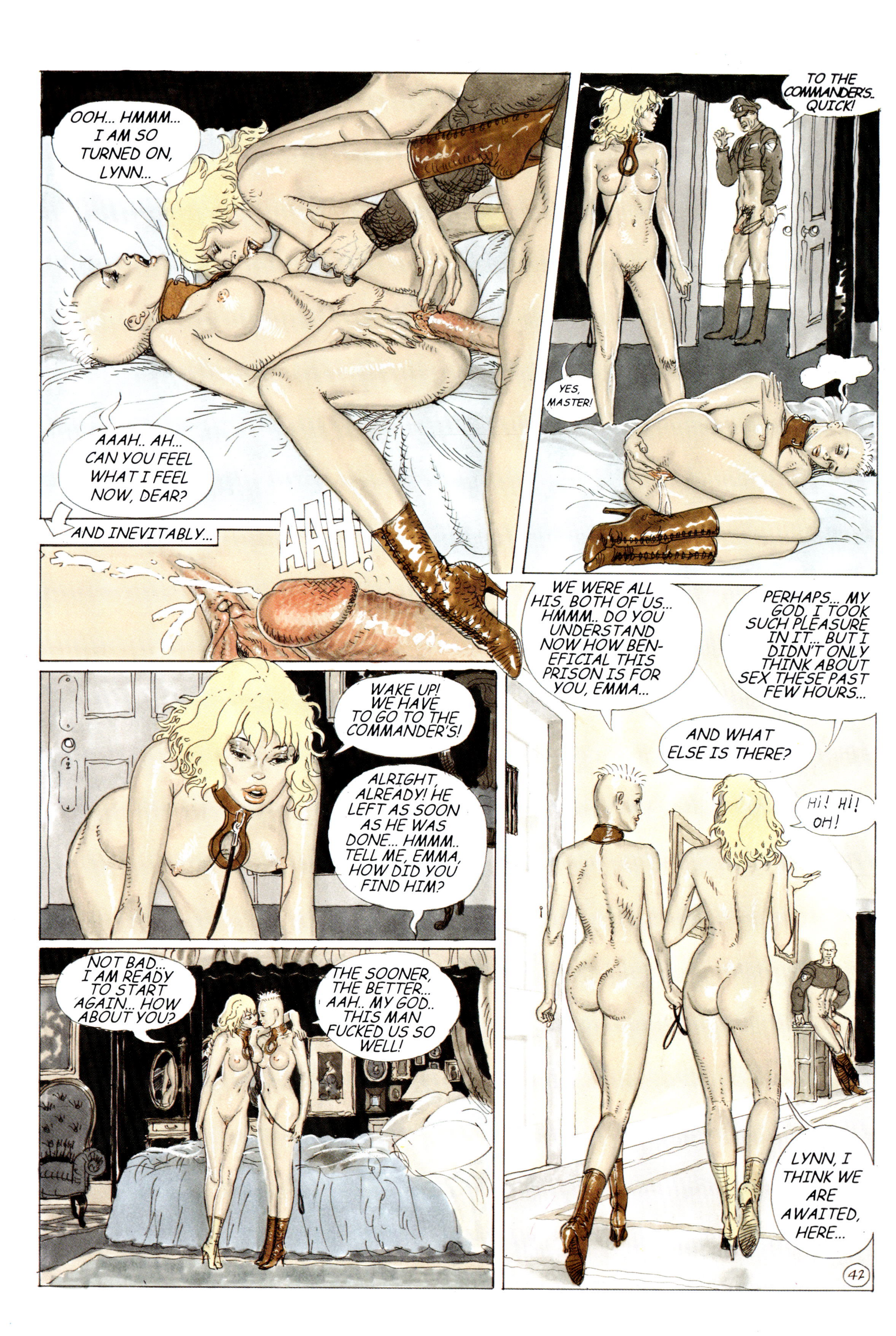
OOH... HMMM... I AM SO TURNED ON, LYNN...
AAAH.. AH... CAN YOU FEEL WHAT I FEEL NOW, DEAR?
TO THE COMMANDER'S.. QUICK!
YES, MASTER!
AND INEVITABLY...
AAH!
WAKE UP! WE HAVE TO GO TO THE COMMANDER'S!
ALRIGHT, ALREADY! HE LEFT AS SOON AS HE WAS DONE... HMMM.. TELL ME, EMMA, HOW DID YOU FIND HIM?
NOT BAD... I AM READY TO START AGAIN... HOW ABOUT YOU?
THE SOONER, THE BETTER... AAH.. MY GOD.. THIS MAN FUCKED US SO WELL!
WE WERE ALL HIS, BOTH OF US... HMMM.. DO YOU UNDERSTAND NOW HOW BENEFICIAL THIS PRISON IS FOR YOU, EMMA...
PERHAPS... MY GOD, I TOOK SUCH PLEASURE IN IT... BUT I DIDN'T ONLY THINK ABOUT SEX THESE PAST FEW HOURS...
AND WHAT ELSE IS THERE?
HI! HI! OH!
LYNN, I THINK WE ARE AWAITED, HERE...

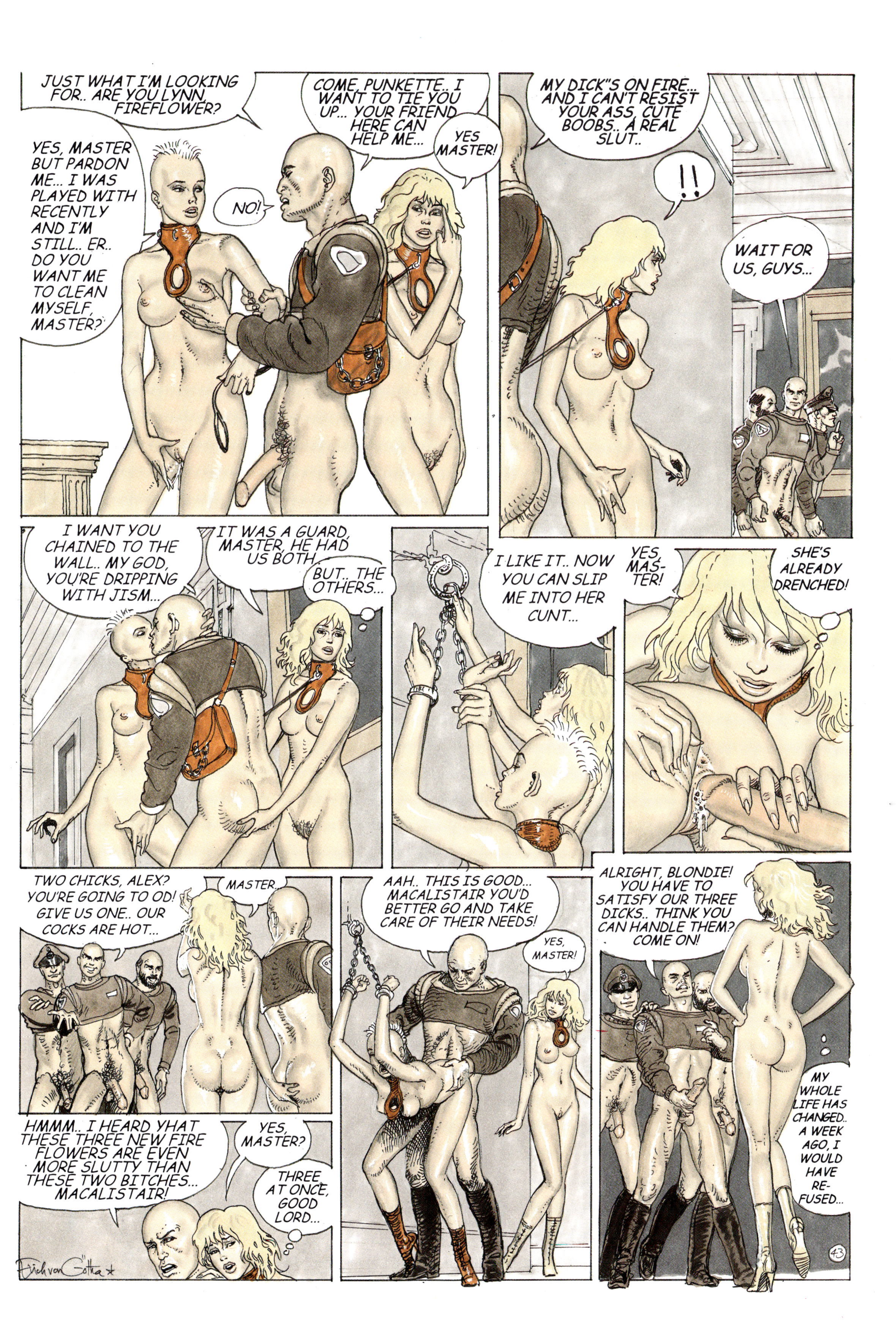

JUST WHAT I'M LOOKING FOR.. ARE YOU LYNN FIREFLOWER?
YES, MASTER BUT PARDON ME... I WAS PLAYED WITH RECENTLY AND I'M STILL.. ER.. DO YOU WANT ME TO CLEAN MYSELF, MASTER?
NO!
COME, PUNKETTE.. I WANT TO TIE YOU UP... YOUR FRIEND HERE CAN HELP ME...
YES MASTER!
MY DICK"S ON FIRE... AND I CAN'T RESIST YOUR ASS, CUTE BOOBS.. A REAL SLUT..
!!
WAIT FOR US, GUYS...
I WANT YOU CHAINED TO THE WALL.. MY GOD, YOU'RE DRIPPING WITH JISM...
IT WAS A GUARD, MASTER, HE HAD US BOTH.
BUT.. THE OTHERS...
I LIKE IT.. NOW YOU CAN SLIP ME INTO HER CUNT...
YES, MAS-TER!
SHE'S ALREADY DRENCHED!
TWO CHICKS, ALEX? YOU'RE GOING TO OD! GIVE US ONE.. OUR COCKS ARE HOT...
MASTER..
HMMM.. I HEARD YHAT THESE THREE NEW FIRE FLOWERS ARE EVEN MORE SLUTTY THAN THESE TWO BITCHES... MACALISTAIR!
YES, MASTER?
THREE AT ONCE, GOOD LORD...
AAH.. THIS IS GOOD... MACALISTAIR YOU'D BETTER GO AND TAKE CARE OF THEIR NEEDS!
YES, MASTER!
ALRIGHT, BLONDIE! YOU HAVE TO SATISFY OUR THREE DICKS.. THINK YOU CAN HANDLE THEM? COME ON!
MY WHOLE LIFE HAS CHANGED.. A WEEK AGO, I WOULD HAVE RE-FUSED...
Erich von Gotha

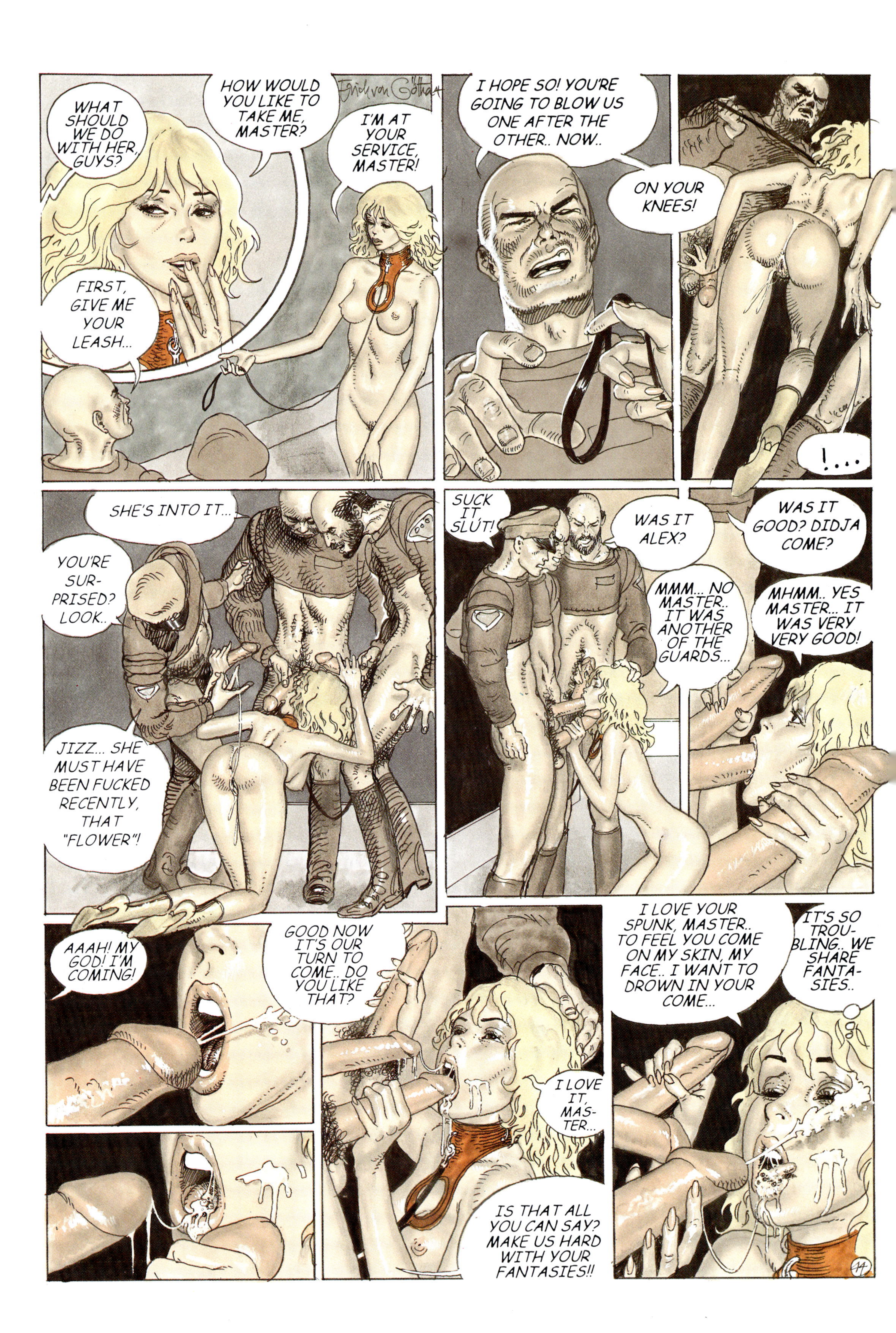
WHAT SHOULD WE DO WITH HER, GUYS?
FIRST, GIVE ME YOUR LEASH...
HOW WOULD YOU LIKE TO TAKE ME, MASTER?
I'M AT YOUR SERVICE, MASTER!
I HOPE SO! YOU'RE GOING TO BLOW US ONE AFTER THE OTHER.. NOW..
ON YOUR KNEES!
!...
SHE'S INTO IT...
YOU'RE SUR-PRISED? LOOK..
JIZZ... SHE MUST HAVE BEEN FUCKED RECENTLY, THAT "FLOWER"!
SUCK IT SLUT!
WAS IT ALEX?
MMM... NO MASTER.. IT WAS ANOTHER OF THE GUARDS...
WAS IT GOOD? DIDJA COME?
MHMM.. YES MASTER... IT WAS VERY VERY GOOD!
AAAH! MY GOD! I'M COMING!
GOOD NOW IT'S OUR TURN TO COME.. DO YOU LIKE THAT?
I LOVE IT, MAS-TER...
IS THAT ALL YOU CAN SAY? MAKE US HARD WITH YOUR FANTASIES!!
I LOVE YOUR SPUNK, MASTER.. TO FEEL YOU COME ON MY SKIN, MY FACE.. I WANT TO DROWN IN YOUR COME...
IT'S SO TROU-BLING.. WE SHARE FANTA-SIES..

...TO FUCK AND BE FUCKED...
AND HOW WOULD YOU LIKE THIS UP YOUR BUTT, SLUT?
I'D LOVE IT, MASTER!

MY TURN, NOW!

THAT'S IT! I'M COMING... AAH!
THEY DRENCHED ME IN SPERM AND STILL I'M SO PROUD OF MYSELF...HMM.. MMM.. DELI-CIOUS...

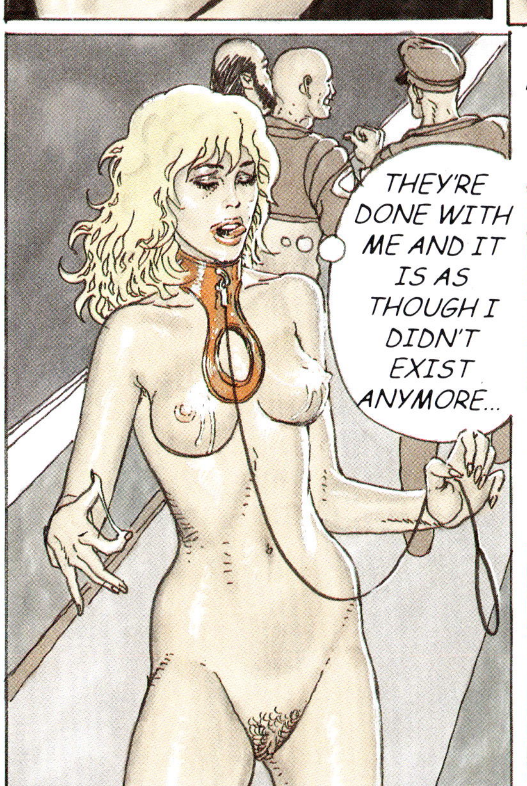
THEY'RE DONE WITH ME AND IT IS AS THOUGH I DIDN'T EXIST ANYMORE...

I AM JUST A FUCKBUCKET... THEY GO AWAY WITH-OUT A LOOK BACK!
STILL, IT'S STRANGE... I FEEL SO CON-TENTED...

HMMM.. THIS FITS YOU PERFECTLY!
TRUE!

LATER...

COME IN!

SLAVE! TONIGHT YOU'LL BE A MODEL FOR MACALISTAIR!
YES, YES, MASTER!

...AND SHE'LL LEARN AT HER EXPENSE...LOOK.. IT'S YOUR FAVORITE TOY, LYNN!
KLIC!

OOH!.. CUTE!..
THIS IS NOT A TOY FOR ME, MASTER...
OF COURSE, IT IS! IT WILL KEEP YOU AWAY FROM TROUBLE, SLAVE... GOOD... COME HERE, MACALISTAIR...
SUCH A DICK!!
OH! SUCH PLEASURE... MMM.. THANK YOU, MASTER... AAH..
THIS BEAUTIFUL BRACELET CONTROLS YOU, SLUT... IT REPORTS ANY THING YOU SAY OR DO, ANYWHERE YOU GO..!
...AND WHATEVER YOU DO THAT DISPLEASES ME... MY LAST RESORT IS TO...
AH.. MY HOLE? ..HEAVENS... AAH.. DEEPER, MASTER...
CLIC!
NO! NOT THE RED BUTTON!
GOOD LORD.. CHOKE.. THE PAIN.. IT IS ATROCIOUS!!
DZZZZ!
THERE! IT'S OVER... NO MORE PAIN IF YOU OBEY MY ORDERS...
AA!!
THE SAME FOR YOUR FRIEND.. REMEMBER THAT SHOULD ANYONE OF YOU BE DISOBEDIENT, YOU WOULD BOTH BE PUNISHED!...
CLIK!
ALSO..SHOULD YOU CALL THE POLICE... OUR POLICE WILL BE PROMPTER!!!
AND WHEN THEY BRING YOU BACK...EH,EH.. YOU WON'T LIKE IT...
DO I REALLY HAVE A CHOICE?..
I... I...
I TRUST YOU, MASTER!..
Erich von Götha

"YES, MASTER" IS ENOUGH!

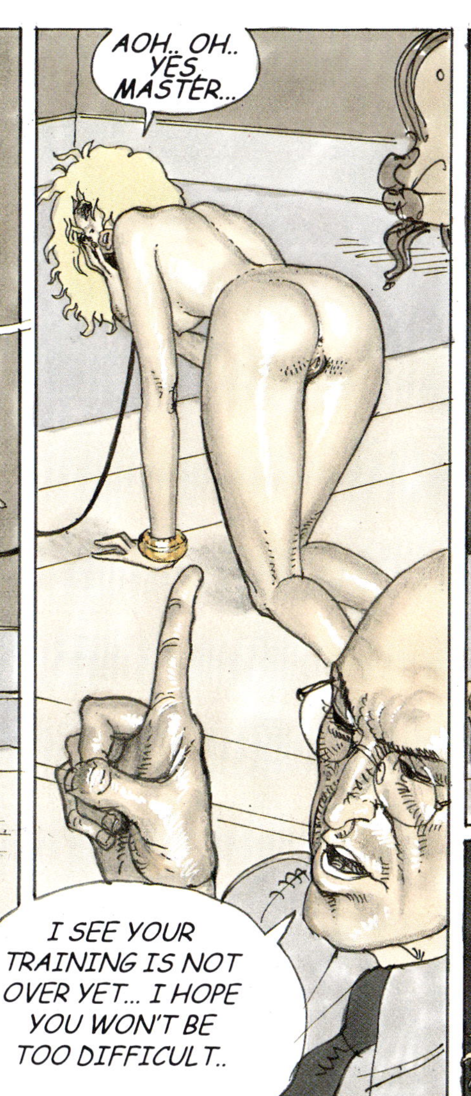
AOH.. OH.. YES, MASTER...
I SEE YOUR TRAINING IS NOT OVER YET... I HOPE YOU WON'T BE TOO DIFFICULT..

I AM SORRY MASTER... I WON'T DO IT AGAIN...
AND HERE I AM AGAIN, CRAWLING IN FRONT OF THIS SADIST...
GOOD.. NOW.. GET DRESSED..

YES, MASTER...

I FEEL MORE EXPOSED THAN WHEN I AM NA-KED...
SO DO I, EMMA... BUT IN YOUR CASE I THINK YOUR BUTT WILL BE EVEN MORE SUCCESFULL!

MAYBE I SHOULD LUBRICATE IT, LITTLE FRIEND...
BUT... I... OÖH..

THIS PLACE, THE ATMO-SPHERE, LYNN.. THIS IS SO STRANGE... I FEEL I AM AT THE WHIM OF ANY-ONE..
THAT'S TRUE, EMMA...

AT THE SAME TIME...
DO YOU REALIZE YOU'LL HAVE TO GO TO JAIL? DO YOU REALLY WANT TO MAKE THAT SACRIFICE? EVEN IF SHE SOMEHOW ESCAPED? DO YOU FOLLOW?
POLIC
YES, MR. PYE! I GOT HER JAILED BUT I DIDN'T KIDNAP HER! I MUST HELP HER!
MEANWHILE...
YOU KNOW, EMMA...
OH!. AH!
I WAS LIKE YOU AT THE BEGINNING.. UNEASY.. BUT NOW, I LOVE IT... THE MORE I GET, THE MORE I WANT...
WEREN'T YOU TURNED ON WHEN THESE THREE BRUTES HAD THEIR WAY WITH YOU.. EMMA?
OF COUSE, YOU BIMBO! I WAS TURNED ON! WHY DOES SHE ASK? WHAT DOES SHE WANT ME TO SAY? DOES SHE WANT TO HEAR HOW WET I WAS?... TELL HER THAT I CAN GET FUCKED BY ALL COMERS?.. AAH.. AAH..
PERSONNALLY, I CAN GET FUCKED BY ALL COMERS!
?
YOU CAN? HA, HA, AH, AH, AH!!
WHY ARE YOU LAUGHING? DID I SAY ANYTHING...
HA! HI! HI! HI!
OH SORRY
HI! HI!
ARE YOU ALL RIGHT? EMMA.. EMMA..
OH, SORRY! TEE HEE...
REMEMBER IT IS DANGEROUS TO DISOBEY!
ER.. YES, YES...
EMMA, WE DON'T HAVE ANY CHOICE... BUT.. YOU AND I CAN HAVE A GOOD TIME! WHAT DO YOU THINK?
IT IS VERY, VERY TEMPTING!
HOW COULD I HAVE IMAGINED THIS CONVERSATION A WEEK AGO... BUT.. WHY NOT?.. MY LIFE IS SO...
WHAT YOU SAID... WE HAVE NO CHOICE!

THE END

PRIAPRISM PRESS

LAST GASP'S EROTIC IMPRINT

NUNS OF TERROR
46 pages color **$12.95**

DISCIPLINE Part 2
48 pages color **$12.95**

TWENTY
62 pages color **$14.95**

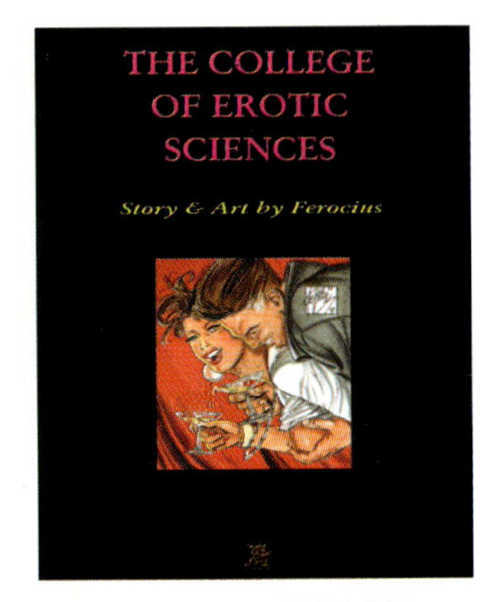

THE COLLEGE OF EROTIC SCIENCES
46 pages color **$12.95**

THE BACKLIST

THE NEW ONE

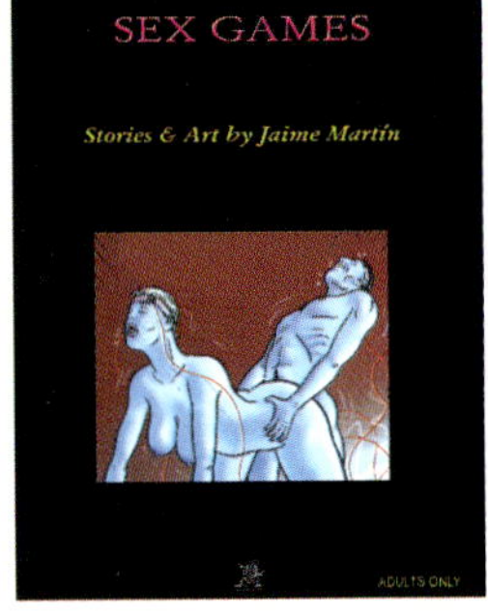

SEX GAMES
s/c 46 pages color **$12.95**

ART BY VON GÖTHA

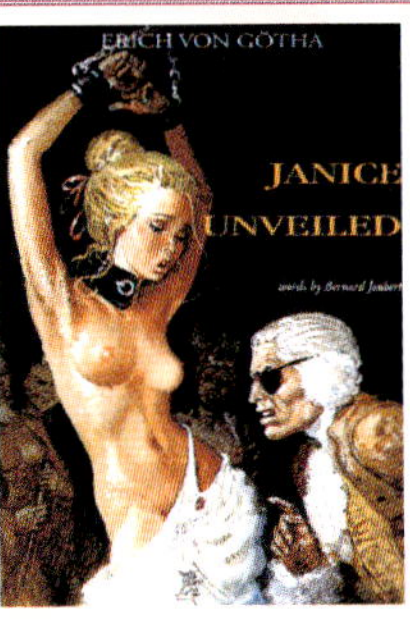

JANICE UNVEILED
h/c color 56 pages **$19.95**

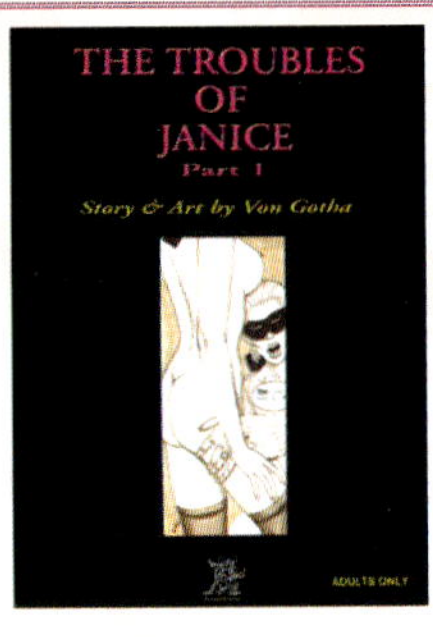

TROUBLE OF JANICE #3
64 pages color **$14.95**

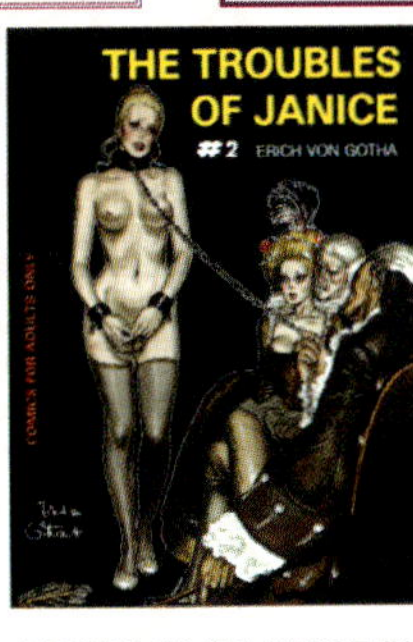

TROUBLES OF JANICE #1
48 pages color **$12.95**

TROUBLES OF JANICE #1
46 pages sepia **$12.95**

NAGARYA Part 1
68 pages color **$15.95**

NAGARYA Part 2
63 pages color **$14.95**

THAMARA & JUDA
62 pages color s/c **$14.95**

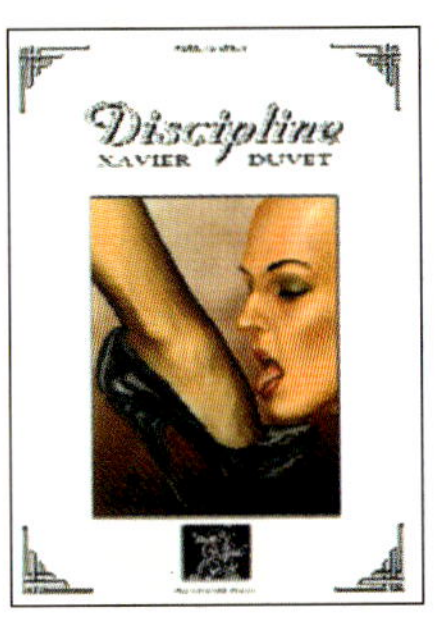

DISCIPLINE Part 1
48 pages color s/c **$12.95**

THE DREAM OF CECILIA
color 48 pages **$12.95**

A VERY SPECIAL PRISON
48 pages color **$12.95**

BONNIE & CLAUDIA
62 pages color **$14.95**

ERIKA
48 pages color **$13.95**

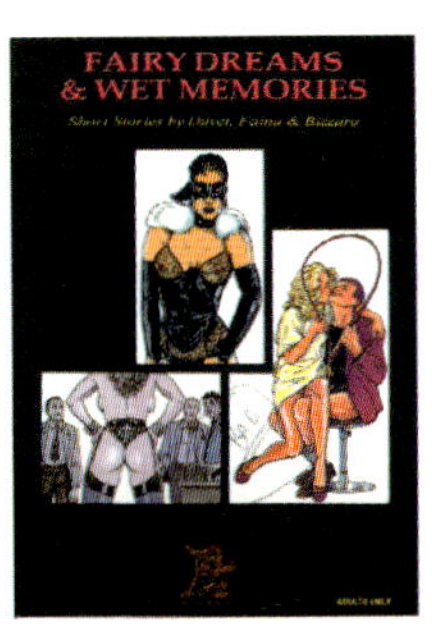

FAIRY DREAMS & WET MEMORIES
62 pages color **$14.95**

SWEET SUBMISSION 2
48 pages b&w **$12.95**

SWEET SUBMISSION
48 pages b&w **$14.95**

**Last Gasp
of San Francisco
P.O. Box 410067
San Francisco
Ca 94141-0067
USA**

lastgasp.com